Not Everybody
Lives the
Same
Way

Jean-Paul Dubois

Not Everybody
Lives the
Same
Way

Translated from the French by
David Homel

MACLEHOSE PRESS
QUERCUS · LONDON

First published as *Tous les hommes n'habitent
pas le monde de la même façon* by Éditions de l'Olivier, Paris, 2019

First published in Great Britain in 2022 by

MacLehose Press
An imprint of Quercus Publishing Ltd
Carmelite House
50 Victoria Embankment
London EC4Y 0DZ

An Hachette UK company

A CIP catalogue record for this book is available from the British Library.

ISBN (HB) 978 1 52940 935 2
ISBN (TPB) 978 1 52941 790 6
ISBN (Ebook) 978 1 52940 936 9

This book is a work of fiction. Names, characters, businesses,
organisations, places and events are either the product of the author's
imagination or used fictitiously. Any resemblance to actual persons,
living or dead, events or locales is entirely coincidental.

2 4 6 8 10 9 7 5 3 1

Designed and typeset in Scala by Patty Rennie
Printed and bound in Great Britain by Clays Ltd, Elcograf S.p.A.

MIX
Paper from
responsible sources
FSC® C104740

Papers used by MacLehose Press are from well-managed
forests and other responsible sources.

For Hélène,
For Tsubaki, Arthur and Louis.
For Vincent Landel, whom I miss.
In memory of Jean-Michel Tarascon and Michel Ramonet.
My attachment to Pascal, boreal gentleman,
and Guy, trans-Canadian sidecar artist.

Lost ten dollars at the track today. What a useless thing.
Rather like jacking-off into a stack of dripping hotcakes.

Charles Bukowski, *On Writing*

The Prison by the River

S NOW HAS BEEN falling for the last week. By the window,
I watch the night and listen to the cold. In this place, the
cold actually makes a noise. A particularly dreadful sound as
if the building, caught in the vice-grip of ice, were crying out
in anguish, in pain, cracking as it contracts. At this time of
night, the prison is sleeping. After a certain amount of experience, once a man grows accustomed to its metabolism, he
can hear it breathing in the dark like a large animal, coughing, swallowing. The prison assimilates and digests us, and
huddling in its belly, hidden in the numbered folds of its
entrails, within the spasms of its gut, we sleep and live the best
we can.

The Montreal penitentiary called Bordeaux, built on the
land of the district with that name, is situated at 800 Gouin
Boulevard West, on the banks of the Rivière des Prairies.
Population: 1,357. Eighty-two inmates were hanged until
the practice was put a stop to in 1962. In the past, before this
universe of constraint was erected, the site must have been
magnificent, with its sprinkling of birch, maple and sumac

trees, and the tall grass laid flat by the paths of wild animals. Nowadays, rats and mice are all that remain of that fauna. True to their uncaring nature, they have invaded this closed world of caged suffering. They are perfectly at ease with detention and their colony has spread through every wing of the building. At night, the rodents are clearly audible in the cells and corridors. To keep them out, we slip rolled-up newspapers and old clothes beneath the doors and in front of the ventilation ducts. To no avail. They pass through, they slip in, they evade and do what they have to.

My cell is called a condo, and it is a step up from the usual kind. The space has earned that ironic label because it boasts a slightly larger floor space than the standard model, which forces what remains of our humanity into approximately six square metres.

Two beds, one atop the other, two windows, two stools bolted to the floor, two shelves, one sink, one toilet.

I share this rectangle with Patrick Horton, a man and a half who has the story of his life tattooed on his back – LIFE'S A BITCH AND THEN YOU DIE – and his love for Harley-Davidsons on the slope of his shoulders and the top of his chest. Patrick is awaiting sentencing after the murder of a Hell's Angel who belonged to the Montreal chapter, shot down on his bike by his friends, who suspected him of cooperating with the police. Patrick is accused of participating in the execution. In view of his intimidating size and affiliation with the biker mafia that boasts an excellent catalogue of murders of all kinds, everyone steps aside with a show of respect when Patrick goes by, the cardinal of Block B. And since it is a known fact that I share the intimacy of his cell, I enjoy the same respect as this tattooed nuncio.

For two nights now, Patrick has been whimpering in his sleep. He has a toothache, with the sharp pain typical of an abscess. He complained about it several times to the guard, who finally brought him some Tylenol. When I asked Patrick why he had not signed up for the dentist's waiting list, he answered, "No way. If you've got a toothache, the sons of bitches won't try and treat it, they'll pull it out. And if you've got two toothaches, they'll pull them both out for you."

We have been cohabiting for nine months now, and things are going well. One of Fate's sly tricks had us arriving here more or less at the same time. Early on, Patrick wanted to know with whom he would have to share a toilet seat. I told him my story, which was quite different from that of the Hell's Angels, who laid a heavy hand on the province's drug traffic, and did not think twice about launching spectacular actions like the ones that produced 160 murders in Quebec between 1994 and 2002, when they faced off against their ancient rivals, the Rock Machine, who themselves were absorbed by the Bandidos, who showed that they deserved their name, but then they, too, fell upon hard times, with eight corpses turning up, all members of the gang, casually distributed in four cars parked side by side, bearing Ontario licence plates.

When Patrick found out why I was in prison, he became interested in my case, like a benevolent master craftsman watching his apprentice's first awkward steps. When I finished my humble tale, he scratched his right earlobe, flaming red with eczema. "When I first laid eyes on you, I wouldn't have thought you had it in you. You did the right thing. No two ways about it. I would have killed him dead."

Maybe that was what I had wanted to do and, according to witnesses, it was what I would have succeeded in doing if six strong-minded people had not combined to stop me. But outside of what I was told, I have only a few images concerning the incident, since my brain seems to have done some selective editing while I was unconscious in the emergency ward.

"Fuck, I would have killed the asshole. Guys like that don't deserve to live."

His fingers tugged at his inflamed ear and he shifted his massive weight from one foot to the other. Tormented by anger, Patrick was ready to go through the wall to finish the job I had left undone. As I watched him bellow and pull at the reddened surface of his skin, I recalled what Serge Bouchard, the anthropologist and specialist in Indigenous Canadian cultures, once said: "Man is a bear that turned out badly."

My wife Winona was Algonquin, and I read a lot of Bouchard to learn about her culture. Back then I was a slow-footed Frenchman who knew almost nothing about the charms of the trembling tent, the mystical rules of the sweat lodge, the foundational legend of the raccoon, the pre-Darwinian reasoning according to which "man is descended from the bear", and the story that tells why "the caribou has white spots only under his mouth".

At that time, prison was just a theoretical concept, a facetious roll of the Monopoly dice ordering you to forgo your turn and spend it in jail. That world clothed in innocence seemed built to last for all eternity, like all the other characters:

my father, Pastor Johanes Hansen, who pulled on the heart-strings of men and the stops of a Hammond organ in his Protestant parish sprinkled with blessed asbestos dust, and Winona Mapachee and her Algonquin sweetness and gentle curves at the controls of her Beaver air taxi as she gently landed, setting down her passengers and her pontoons on the water of countless northern lakes, and my dog Nouk, who had just been born and seemed to gaze at me with her big black eyes as if I were the beginning and end of all things.

Yes, I loved those days, so distant now, when all three were alive.

I wish I could sleep. And not hear the rats. Not breathe the smell of men. Not listen to winter through a pane of glass. Not have to eat brown chicken boiled in greasy water. Not run the risk of getting beaten to death for a misspoken word or a handful of tobacco. Not be forced to piss in the sink because, after curfew, we are not allowed to flush the toilet. Not see, every evening, Patrick drop his trousers, sit down on the seat, and defecate as he praises his Harley's dual forks, which, as it idled, "shivered like it was the middle of winter". During every session, he does his duty with a peaceful attitude and talks to me with such an astonishing sense of calm that his mouth and mind seem completely detached from his rectal concerns. He does not even try to modulate his flatulence. As he finishes up, Patrick goes on enlightening me about the reliability of the latest engines mounted on silent blocks, then readjusts his britches like a man knocking off work for the day, laying a spotless towel over the seat which is meant to act as a cover, but reminds me of the end of the service, *Ite, missa est.*

Close my eyes. Sleep. The only way to get out of here and leave the rats behind.

During the summer, if I stood at the edge of the left-hand window, I could see the waters of the Rivière des Prairies flowing swiftly towards two islands, Bourdon and Bonfoin, and the great Saint Lawrence that would swallow up the smaller river. But that night, nothing. The snow had whited everything out, even the darkness.

Patrick did not know it, but sometimes, at the evening hour, Winona, Johanes and Nouk would come and visit. They would enter, and I could see them as clearly as all the squalor this cell contained. They would speak, they were here, close by. Ever since I lost them, years ago, they have come and gone in my thoughts, at home there. They say what is on their minds, go about their business, try and repair the disorder of my life and sometimes find the words that can ease me into sleep and the peace of the evening. Each in their own way, with their particular roles and attributes, they support me and never judge. Especially when I ended up in prison. They did not know any more than I did how it happened, nor why everything turned upside down so fast, in a matter of days. They were not there to unearth the origin of my misfortune. They were simply striving to recreate our family.

During the first years, I had enormous difficulty accepting the fact that I would have to live with the dead. Listening to my father's voice without flinching, as I did when I was a boy, when we lived in Toulouse and my mother loved us. As for

Winona, my disturbance lifted quickly, for she had prepared me for the legend of the Algonquin infra-world where the living and the dead stand side by side. She often said there was nothing more normal than engaging in dialogue with the departed, who were now living in another universe. "Our ancestors pursue another existence. We bury them with all their things so they can continue their activities elsewhere." I loved the fragile logic of that world cobbled together with hope and love. We equipped their departed owners with their tools, and they were supposed to go on functioning, even if they were electric, whatever the amps and plugs were in the invisible world. As for my dog Nouk, who knew everything about time, men and the laws of winter, a dog who could read us like a book, she came and stretched out close by me as she had always done. Without the intercession of sha-mans, trusting her memory of my smell, she would find me. After exploring the shadows, she went back to her spot and lay down by me, continuing our life together where we had left off.

I was incarcerated in Bordeaux Prison the very day Barack Obama was elected, November 4, 2008. For me it was a long and trying day with my transfer to the courthouse, the wait-ing in the corridor, my appearance before Judge Lorimier, who, despite his seemingly benevolent questioning, seemed preoccupied by a chattering crowd of personal concerns, the phantom plea of my depressive lawyer, who called me "Jans-sen", inventing "heavy psychiatric baggage" for me, and who gave the impression he had just happened upon my case, either that or he was arguing someone else's, then the verdict pronounced by Lorimier, who chewed and swallowed his words, the quantum of the sentence, two years without parole, quickly forgotten in the memory of the courtroom, the deluge of rain during the return trip, the traffic jams, the arrival at the prison, identification, the unpleasant search, three in a cell as big as a closet, "shut your trap, here you shut your trap", a mattress on the floor, rat droppings, used Kleenex scattered here and there, a vague smell of urine, the meal tray, brown chicken, black night.

A month before Barack Obama officially settled into the White House, I was transferred to my new lodgings, the condo that Patrick Horton and I still share. The move freed me from the hellish entrails of Block A, where violent assaults set the tone for the day and even the night. Though an incident can always occur here, thanks to Patrick's pedigree and stature, life is more tolerable. And when the weight of being myself and the refusal of time to move forward become too heavy a burden, I simply give up and give in to the slow stubborn beat of the prison clock, and submit to the schedule of its "daily regimen": "7.00 a.m., cells open. 7.30 a.m., breakfast served. 8.00 a.m., sectorial activities. 11.15 a.m., lunch served. 1.00 p.m., sectorial activities. 4.15 p.m., dinner served. 6.00 p.m., sectorial activities. 10.30 p.m., lights out and cells closed. Smoking prohibited inside and outside the establishment. Also prohibited: game consoles, mobile phones, pornographic photographs. Beds must be made by 8.00 a.m. and cells cleaned every morning by 9.00 a.m."

.   .   .

It is a very strange sensation to have been put in a box and stripped of all responsibility. For twenty-six years, in the Ahuntsic district, less than a kilometre from the prison – at the beginning it was terribly troubling to be locked up so close to home – I practised the very demanding trade of superintendent, a combination of magician and jack-of-all-trades, a top-drawer factotum who could restore and repair a whole little world of specialised operations, a complex universe made of cables, tubes, pipes, junctions, derivations, columns, traps and dating devices, a playful little world always eager to go haywire, create problems and induce breakdowns that had to be solved immediately with a reservoir of memory, knowledge, technique, observation and sometimes plain dumb luck. In the apartment building called the Excelsior, I was a sort of *deus ex machina* to whom the place was entrusted, along with the maintenance, surveillance and good conduct of the condo and its sixty-eight units. The residents owned their apartments and enjoyed the use of a yard planted with trees and bushes, a heated pool filled with 230,000 litres of water purified with salt, an underground parking garage with an area for washing cars, a gym, a lobby with a waiting room and reception desk, a space for meetings called "the Forum", twenty-four surveillance cameras, and three lifts of generous capacity supplied by the Kone company.

For twenty-six years, I carried out this Herculean task, both stimulating and exhausting. The work was never over, and practically invisible since it consisted mainly of maintaining sixty-eight units in perfect balance despite the erosion of time, the climate and obsolescence. Nine thousand, five hundred days of watchfulness, vigilance, involvement; nine thousand, five hundred days of investigation, verification, trips up to the roof, excursions to every floor; one hundred and four seasons during which I went beyond the call of duty to help seniors, console widows, visit the sick, and even watch over the dead, since that did happen twice.

My father Johanes Hansen was a Protestant pastor, and I believe the education he gave me had much to do with the sense of abnegation I displayed during those years of keeping the ship afloat. To practise in that way, in the shadows, every day carrying out humble tasks with serious intent and attention to detail, seems completely in the spirit of the Reformation such as Johanes defended in his churches.

I know nothing of the man who, after me, took on the burden and agreed to live in the bowels of the Excelsior. And nothing of what those bowels look like today. I know only that the small imaginative world of sixty-eight units, with its capacity to produce infinite combinations of breakdowns, concerns and puzzles to solve, is something I miss enormously.

At times, I would speak to the objects and machines, and I believed they could understand me in return. Today, all I have is Patrick, his rotten tooth and his dual forks.

I, who once administered and assured the good conduct of the Excelsior, am now forced to fit into the emollient "life regimen" of my new condo: 8.00 a.m., sectorial activities. 4.15 p.m., dinner served. 9.00 p.m., biker stools. 10.30 p.m., lights out and cells closed.

. . .

This morning, when he awoke, Patrick called the guard and asked for an emergency appointment with the dentist. Patrick dreaded him more than a midnight raid from the Bandidos. His cheek had swelled up during the night and the pain turned him into a stripped wire. He paced the cell like a wasp caught in a jar. "Would it bug you too much to make my bed this morning? This fucking tooth is killing me. I got that from my father. His teeth were rotten, too. It's genetic, that's what they tell you. What did you say? I have no idea, don't bust my balls with your stupid questions, you think I'm in the mood? They say he looks just like Nicholson playing that crazy guy. What time is it? That asshole must be at home, jerking off into his cornflakes. Let me tell you, he'd better treat me first class, and if he doesn't, take it from me, I'm going to kick that son of a bitch's ass. Shit! What time is it?"

For Patrick, especially when his molar is hurting him, the world is divided into two distinct categories of individuals. Those who know and appreciate the siren song of Harley-Davidson dual forks. And the rest, much more numerous, philistines when it comes to Isolastics, who need to have their asses kicked.

In two hours' time, I have an appointment with a certain Gaëtan Brossard, a penitentiary administration official whose job is to review files for sentence reduction before transferring them to the judge. I met Brossard once, three or four months ago. His appearance has something calming about it, and his face cut from Viggo Mortensen cloth adds to his role as benevolent gatekeeper.

Our first meeting was of short duration. He had not even opened the file that contained my trial documents.

"Today's meeting is purely a formality, just a way of establishing contact, Mr Hansen. Considering the serious crimes you have committed, I am unfortunately unable to examine or consider, at this point, any possibility of parole, or even a day pass. We will meet again in several months, and if your conduct is satisfactory, we can perhaps look at some solutions."

Brossard has not changed his modus operandi. I notice a detail I missed the first time. When he is not speaking, he has a way of sniffing his fingertips. With each breath, his nostrils dilate, and then, reassured no doubt by the recognition of familiar molecules, they go back to their normal dimensions.

"I will be frank with you, Mr Hansen. Your evaluations are excellent in all areas and would seem to indicate a transfer of your file to the judge, and a favourable outcome. However, you must first convince me that you have understood the seriousness of your acts and that you regret them with full awareness. Do you regret what you did, Mr Hansen?"

No doubt I should have said what he was waiting to hear, beg the world's pardon, express deep and sincere remorse, formulate a farandole of regrets, admit that what happened that day was incomprehensible, ask forgiveness from the victim for the suffering I inflicted, and, at the end of my act of contrition, lower my head with the weight of shame.

I did nothing of the sort. Not a single word issued from my mouth. Nothing. My features remained as inexpressive as an iron mask, and it took all my strength not to admit to this Viggo Mortensen character that my most sincere regret was not having had more time and more strength to break every bone in the body of that contemptible bastard, repugnant and full of himself.

"I was expecting something different from you, Mr Hansen. A more appropriate reaction. It is obvious when I read the reports on you, when I examine your life story and your past, it is clear to me that you don't belong here. Yet I am afraid that due to your persistent refusal to re-evaluate your own behaviour, you will be obliged to remain here for some time longer. And that is what's regrettable, Mr Hansen. Every day you spend in this prison is a day too many. Is someone waiting for you on the outside?"

How could I explain to him that no-one was waiting for me on the outside? But that in this very room where we sat – and I could feel their breath upon me – Winona, Johanes and Nouk were with me, patient and polite, and had been here for some time as they waited for him to leave.

Still under the influence of the local anaesthetic, leaking reddish saliva onto a paper towel, Patrick returned from his dental appointment. His encounter with Nicholson apparently went badly.

"That bastard pulled it right out. I knew it, fuck, they'd warned me. But the bastard gave me no choice. He said he couldn't do anything to save my tooth, and besides, I had an enormous abscess. He showed me some shit on an X-ray and told me, 'See, it's really infected.' 'Don't bust my balls,' I answered. 'Do what you have to, but I'm telling you, if you hurt me, you're dead.' With all the stuff he shot into my gums, there must have been enough to put the whole village where I was born to sleep. I don't know when I'm going to get out of here, but I swear, the minute I'm free, I'm going straight to that bastard's place and I'm going to kick his ass."

Tonight, the forecast is for minus twenty-eight Celsius, with a wind chill of minus thirty-four. Christmas is in four days. Nicholson will celebrate the occasion with his family, all of them with impeccable dentition, whitened by the paterfamilias. The youngest daughter will be wearing braces and her mother will promise that this winter will be her last with a mouthful of metal. A full spectrum of ridiculous ornaments and lights will sparkle and blink throughout the house as in all the houses of the city, the department stores will play Christmas carols to grease the customers' credit cards, and in a senseless ballet, all sorts of useless and expensive objects, pulled from the void and soon to return there, will transit from one hand to the next while, for the occasion, enchanted radio frequencies will programme "All I Want for Christmas Is You".

But in here, a low-cost priest will rush through a standard-issue mass for people who love to genuflect, and, without believing a word of it, he will promise us that one day we will sit at the right hand of our Creator. Then he will head for the door to breathe in the juvenile perfume of choir boys. Meanwhile, we miscreants, impious, occasional bandits and muscle-bound criminals will be treated to a double portion of brown chicken and gravy accompanied by a spongy object made of expired maple cream. As I dig in, with all good intent, I will wish Patrick Merry Christmas. As he chews on his submissive fowl, he will tell me, "Don't bust my balls with your Christmas shit."

Skagen, the Church Buried in Sand

I WAS BORN in Toulouse, in the Clinique des Teinturiers, on February 20, 1955, at ten in the evening. In the room I was assigned, two people I had never seen watched me sleep. The young woman lying next to me, who seemed to be coming back from an evening out, stunningly beautiful, smiling, relaxed despite the labour of childbirth, was Anna Margerit, my mother. She was twenty-five. The man sitting next to her, trying not to put too much weight on the edge of the bed, tall with blond hair and pale blue eyes full of benevolence and kindness, was Johanes Hansen, my father. He was thirty. Both appeared satisfied with the finished product, initiated in circumstances whose consequences they might not have been aware of at the time. My parents had chosen my first names long before my birth. I would be Paul Christian Frederic Hansen. Hard to get more Danish than that. Born into the culture, its blood flowing in my veins, everything you could desire, starting with serendipity, I would all the same bear French citizenship.

Like his four brothers, Johanes was born in Jutland, in the town of Skagen, with its eight thousand inhabitants, located at the northernmost tip of Denmark, where fish is spoken exclusively from birth onwards. Fishermen from generation to generation, the Hansens contributed to the quiet prosperity of the town, which seemed to cling to the earth to keep from drifting towards the nearby coasts of Kristiansand, in Norway, or Gothenburg, in Sweden. As the world changed habits and priorities, some of the Hansen brothers adapted to new ways and sold their fishing boats to specialise in fishmeal processing. Thor, the eldest, continued to sail among the reefs of the dangerous waters that tourists liked to admire from the tip of Grenen when, with the weather at its worst, the ancestral conflict between the currents of the Baltic and those of the North Sea stirred anew.

Johanes belonged to that slender minority of Hansens, the branch of the *der bør i landet*, "those who live on the land". Very early in his life, my father turned his back on the sea. He preferred to contemplate the peninsula's special luminosity, which attracted the greatest painters of the country, who created, with style and perseverance, the famous Skagen school. Paintings of peaceful landscapes, simple men and women at work, the North Sea in its fusion, boats on the Baltic, nothing that would shake the doors of the museums or ruffle feathers at the art schools. Just beautiful canvases faithfully worked, made for the people of this country, who did not ask for more.

Besides being a *bør i landet*, in his twelfth year my father took up religion, a sport that until then had been totally neglected by the family. Much later, he told me of the unusual circumstances that led him to become a pastor. It is a story of sand, shifting sand, driven by history and the wind.

In the fourteenth century, at the northernmost point of the peninsula, at the edge of the town, a church dedicated to the patron saint of sailors was built a few steps from the sea. Forty-five metres long, with a 22-metre-high gabled bell tower, and thirty-eight rows of pews, it was an imposing building unique in all Jutland. No doubt too exposed to the sea spray, too close to the breath of the storms, helpless in the face of the wind, for soon the building began to suffer from earth sickness, and, beginning around 1770, sand gradually invaded first the parvis, then the nave, the hungry dunes working night and day to nibble away and push back the walls of the church. In 1775, a terrible storm blocked the entrances and the good citizens had to dig tunnels in order to worship at their temple. They continued to do this for another twenty years, clearing the walls and exits, week after week. But the wind kept blowing and the sand kept piling up. One day, overwhelmed, admitting defeat, God gave up the struggle and the clergy closed the church for good after selling its furniture at auction. Today, sand has completely covered the building. Only eighteen metres of the bell tower still emerge from the dunes.

The sight of this buried church, this wreckage of faith, gave my father the will to become a pastor. "You see, at the time I thought I had no faith, I didn't even know what that meant. I felt a purely aesthetic emotion as I looked upon this unique and moving sight, the kind of thing you see only once in a lifetime. A true canvas of the Skagen school. If on that day, in its place, I had seen a station covered by sand, with only the gable and the clock tower visible, perhaps I would have become a railwayman." Such was my father. *Bør i landet* certainly, but most of all aware of the need to navigate constantly through the permanence of doubt, at times attracted by the fragile sail of an abandoned church, other times drawn by the robust and adventurous life of the railways.

My mother, Anna Madeleine Margerit, travelled to Skagen twice. There she met the entire Hansen tribe, men and women built identically to withstand the rigours of the climate, and live that way for centuries. They prepared her plaice with stewed currants and cranberries, smoked eel, *pramdragergryde*, she drank a sip of *akavit*, then made the pilgrimage to the church choked by sand, where she photographed my father with the other extant Hansens lined up in front of the remains of the bell tower. On the way back, she spoke to my father of how she felt when she saw this liturgical vestige emerge from the earth. "How could you have wanted to be a pastor after seeing something like that? It evokes nothing but impotence, abandonment, the surrender of God and the Church. If I were you, I would have joined my brothers, married a local woman, and spent my time grinding fish to bits." Apparently, according to Anna, my father nodded his head slowly before confessing with his clergyman's smile, "I agree with you, except for the question of marrying a woman who looks like my brothers."

Anna Madeleine Margerit was born in Toulouse. Her parents, whom I never knew, ran a small cinema, modestly called Le Spargo – from the Latin, "I sow". At the time it sported the brand-new label of "repertory", where only high-brow films such as *Les Gauloises bleues*, *Blow-Up*, *Theorem* and *Zabriskie Point* were shown. Imbued from childhood with these images, raised in the lap of interminable credits, poignant scores, outrageous kisses and abstruse dramas, my mother became an encyclopedia of cinema. She knew every nook and cranny of this world and was able to name the editor of a Pabst film, the composer of a Hawks masterpiece and the lighting designer of an Epstein offering. Generally speaking, she was more interested in film trades, the makers, the directors, the producers, than in the all-too-predictable know-how of the actors.

In April 1960 in Toulouse, the Hansens looked like the best and most conventional family of the times. A measured and attentive husband, brimming with charm, speaking clear, polished French, though spiced with a light, exotic Nordic accent, having acquired a spot as the second pastor at the old church on the rue Pargaminières, and unanimous approval for his preaching and his practice. A wife who seemed to be in love with her husband, combining natural beauty that everyone agreed was spectacular with equally impressive intellectual gifts, dividing her time between bringing up her son and programming a repertory cinema, sharing the management with her parents until 1958. As for young Paul Christian Frederic, though too soon to judge as he toddled along his way, he did what he was asked to do when he was asked to do it, and mastered the catalogue of polite greetings as he accompanied his father to church every Sunday to listen to him hold forth about the ways of the world and its sinful weaknesses.

My mother was impervious to the Church and to faith and resisted the very idea of sin. She never put so much as a toe, let alone a foot, inside the house of the Lord. That was the only shadow of a blemish in this still life that the Skagen school would have certainly neglected. Given that, why did she agree to share her life with a young Protestant pastor? When, much later, I questioned my mother about this, I always received the same answer, one that both intrigued and reassured me. "Your father is so handsome."

Yet at times he would get carried away. At the table, when voices rose between them, my father would reach for the urticating fetish mantra he was so fond of. "May you live, if only for a few hours, in the perfection of faith." Later I understood what Anna Madeleine must have felt. That unbearably honeyed and softly condescending benevolence always produced the same reaction. "How can you say such crap?"

I sincerely believe that in this first posting, eager to please and create superficial unanimity, Pastor Hansen, my father, showed himself to be conventional, disappointing, a man of dull platitudes. But was he really being asked for anything else?

I can also say that at the time, despite the small scrapes of everyday life, my parents were happy to share their lives. I never knew and still do not know what their original togetherness was based on. Despite the few questions I asked that very quickly provoked embarrassment and discomfort, I never knew where or in what circumstances my father and mother met, nor by what mischievous wrinkle of amorous destiny a native of Skagen, dug out from under his dunes, and a lady devotee from an upmarket movie theatre managed, in 1953, to bridge the 2,420 kilometres that separated them, leap the language barrier, and make rich use of the clever trick they had played on life.

Five years later, in 1958, death came into our family for the first time. On a summer's night, the victim of a terrible impact, Anna's parents' black Citroën DS 19 disintegrated on one of the most beautiful secondary routes in the southern part of the country, lined with majestic plane trees, whose summits joined together in an arch, and wove a delicate, protective umbrella with their wide crowns.

My grandparents were returning from the Festival de la Cité in Carcassonne. In the heat of the evening, imprisoned behind the famous towers and ramparts, they had gone to see *La Chanson de Roland*, an epic of four thousand lines, performed and directed by Jean Deschamps. "Carle our most noble Emperor and King, Hath tarried now full seven years in Spain." Perhaps they died with those words in their heads, the verses bouncing around their skulls as one impact was followed by another, the scansion stuck and clinging to their memories, like the loop of a broken record.

Around 1 a.m., the phone rang, and a surge of pain and sorrow swept through the apartment. Naturally, everything I relate here was told to me later by my parents, for I retained no images or sounds that would speak of those moments, though they shook our family to the core.

In Naurouze, where the waters of the Canal du Midi divide between the Atlantic and the Mediterranean, the Citroën left its path and crashed head-on into a plane tree. The car literally exploded against the trunk, launching its fibreglass roof into the ditches of a nearby field and the bodies of my grandparents in the other direction, onto a plot of land on the other side of the road.

In this hamlet where the waters flow and part, at this point where worlds divide, there are two huge stones, separated only by a few centimetres. Legend has it that when these stones touch, the end of the world will be nigh.

That night they maintained their position, though the Margerit family entered the end of days. They were buried according to Catholic rites after a service celebrated in Saint Étienne cathedral, which, of course, my father attended, moved no doubt, but certainly attentive to the pomp and circumstance of the funeral, the trickery of the liturgy and the sleights of hand of the competition.

The Spargo lost those who had created it, but inherited a new full-time administrator, my mother, who seemed ready and willing to write a new chapter of its history.

The year 1958 was a good one for the Spargo. *Mon Oncle*, *Vertigo*, *Touch of Evil* and *Cat on a Hot Tin Roof* filled the seats for several weeks and helped the audience forget about the worn velvet and the hard armrests. Anna had a new Philips projector installed, as well as a xenon lamp, an improved sound system and a screen with better reflectivity. With these updates, the little Spargo boasted of a new look, at least inside. The cosmetic concerns would come later.

Like small cinemas, places of worship were living their last hurrah. The world was changing, and though the upheaval was just beginning, my father had to fight, writing and rewriting his sermons to retain an audience eager to discover and experience other less conventional and more permissive distractions.

By my tenth year, anyone who cared to pay heed could hear the hinges of the old world giving way. We lived on the quai Lombard in an old apartment with ceilings that reached the stratosphere. Its wide windows equipped with wooden venetian blinds gave onto the river, whose colours changed with the seasons. During the summer, old plane trees shaded the evenings, and at night you could scarcely hear the waters of the Garonne.

The Pierre-de-Fermat College was not very far from the river and our house, but much too close, for my liking, to the church where my father officiated. I would have died rather than let anyone know that the big-boned charmer running down the steps of that strange-looking building at the end of the street, in his impeccable grey clergyman's suit, was my father. At the college, as far as everyone knew, he was a fish-meal importer. Amen to that. I confessed this little lie to him and begged him not to deny it if ever he was questioned about the subject. "You should not be ashamed of your father's work. There is nothing to hide. On the contrary. In Denmark, children of pastors are very proud of their fathers."

From that day on, my mother took over the administration of my schooling and met with my teachers to deal with the affairs of the day. Johanes never mentioned the subject again. But one evening I found a note he had put on my desk. I was still a child, and when I read the words, I felt great confusion and vague sadness, the origin of which I could not locate.

My father had written, "I am just a little boy enjoying himself, shadowed by a Protestant pastor who is bothering him. André Gide."

On December 31, around eight in the evening, a violent battle involving a dozen inmates from rival gangs broke out in our sector's passageway, and we were all subjected to the lockdown procedure. Ambulances drove into the main yard of the prison to cart away two belligerents with serious knife wounds. The little festivities organised for the end of the year were cancelled.

At midnight, when most of us were in bed, we began to hear the distant hammering of a metal object against a cell door. It was a heavy, insistent, repetitive sound that echoed through the empty corridors. Another one joined the first. Then a third, and within a minute, the entire sector echoed with the commotion, and soon all the prisoners from the other wings were part of it. It was like the beating of an enormous steel heart rising up to heaven. The canticle of the banished making their wishes known. I had never heard such a thing. Patrick, like a devil, drunk with power, was hell-bound to break through the wall he knew would resist. He stared at it, smiled and bludgeoned it with all his might. Seeing him at work in the midst of the uproar gave me goosebumps. All of us were beating away in unison on different things. Our personal sufferings. The contempt we were made to endure. Our absent families. Flippant judges, hurried dentists, a whole ill-defined world that Patrick Horton, sooner or later, would split open with a switchblade. On that first night of the year 2010, we had become a horde of caged beasts drumming in the jaded belly of that ice-bound prison on the edge of the frozen river.

Little by little, as if an invisible hand were lowering the sound potentiometer, the beating subsided, then disappeared into darkness.

That night, there were no rounds. The guards kept to themselves, and we were left with the quantum of our sentences. Minus one year.

Today is January 3, 2010. Tomorrow will mark fourteen months that I have been locked up here. Patrick is drawing. From behind, he looks like a child concentrating on his work, applying himself to reproduce a fragment of the world with all its shapes and colours. Patrick draws a lot. Naive compositions, landscapes, faces and, of course, motorcycles that he tries to recreate as realistically as possible. Sometimes, like a schoolboy, he will trace his subjects, and then spend an hour or two copying and colouring them in with pencils. Seeing this murderous hulk give the best of himself to these childish tasks has a touching side, but it also causes me great distress, for it raises many questions about the shitty meanderings of the human soul.

"I was thinking about that business with the shrink the other day. You got it all wrong." On his sheet of paper, carefully following the tenuous thread of his drawing, Patrick instructs me on proper behaviour with an evaluator. "There's nothing to it. Just tell him what he wants to hear. Keep it simple. I regret to death what I did. I recognise that I went too far. I have no excuse. I had great fucking parents who didn't raise me that way. I think prison has done me good. I've learned respect here and gotten back on the straight and narrow. I think I'm ready to get out there and get some real training. I'd like to be a bus driver. If you're not in the mood for the bus, replace it with something else. You want the joker to be happy, so he'll feel like you're pulling yourself up by your bootstraps and getting ready to serve. Understand? The rule is very simple. You have to convince him you've got no balls. Throw me the eraser. Fuck, when I talk, I always go over the line."

When you add together all his sentences in his still young life, Patrick Horton has already served five years in prison. As for me, I do not know when I will get out of here. Two years in prison for the offence I committed seems fitting, equal to the seriousness of the crime. Which is, in my opinion, neither heinous nor trivial. But in my case, one major problem prevents me from applying Horton's Theorem. I have no problem openly regretting and deploring my action, insofar as it was committed against an ordinary citizen, but I find it totally justified when it comes to the particular victim I assaulted. To hell with the evaluator – for that man, there will never be mercy or pardon.

Patrick's painful abscess is now just an unpleasant memory. But every night before brushing his teeth, he insists on showing me the hole that the extraction left in his gum. "I wonder what that damn tooth is doing now. It was my tooth, after all. Even if it was rotten, it was mine. Plus it had a crown on it. The doctor should have given it back to me. I paid a shit-load for the fucking ceramics. If they want, they can recycle it and make other teeth or something else. What do you think?"

I like Patrick well enough, but he is unpredictable, and sometimes he expresses crazy ideas and wields totally insane concepts. A few days before Christmas, I watched him engage in a long and serious conversation with one of our guards, who seemed to subscribe to the same way of thinking, and explain that he had a buddy who could bend forks from a distance. The guard seemed bewitched, and Patrick acted out the scene, claiming he had witnessed the utensil twisting on the table like spaghetti. "It's called psychokinesis. I read up about it. My pal has been practising it for years. He can't actually move things, I mean, make them go one way or the other. That's impossible. But he can twist stuff. As long as it's not too thick. A spoon or a fork, no problem. But a screwdriver, for example, he can't do that. A couple times I watched him focus on a fucking screwdriver. He spent an hour on it, maybe two. But no go. He ended up dead, exhausted, covered in sweat. His wife has to hide the screwdrivers from him. I read that in India there was a guy like him who could open fridge doors and make bicycle wheels spin."

Over time, I have gotten used to Patrick's strange excesses, his unpredictable flashes that burn out just as quickly if there isn't adequate fuel or a sympathetic listener.

At this time of the year, night falls around four-thirty. More or less dinner hour, very little in our bowls and fewer words on our tongues. A mist of melancholy descends, and offers protection for those who seek isolation. These are the bad hours of the day, late afternoon when people on the outside are happy to return home after leaving work, braving the snow and cold. At the Excelsior, I would leave my duties and wait for

Winona in the apartment. Often we would go walking with Nouk in Ahuntsic Park. Free of all constraints, we floated in time, in complete possession of our lives, throwing off carefree molecules of happiness with every step, while the dog covered her white fur in coats of snow. Sometimes I close my eyes and try to recreate those evening strolls in the Garden of Eden, but every time I try, savage voices erupt in the corridors and cells, and bring down the patient, fragile construction my memory is trying to build. That is when a man takes the measure of what a prison sentence is. The chronic inability to escape, if only for the time he needs to take a walk with the dead.

I said they could visit me here. But I can never join them on the outside.

Now it is Patrick's hour, the routine I cannot get used to. He removes the cloth from the bowl, unzips his pants, sits down and stares at me, pushing hard, making the veins in his face stand out. The sound of a pebble dropping into deep water announces the end of the first delivery. "I still don't know when I'll go to court for my case. I'm thinking maybe I should change lawyers. I don't like the one I have. He looks like he belongs in a boy band with those tassel loafers he wears. I swear to God. The last time, the jerk showed up in front of the judge with tassel slip-ons and cheerleader socks." Then silence, accompanied by another session of pushing, a pebble, he exhales, a slack expression on his face. "I'm going to get rid of the joker, I can't stand him. What I need is a brute, a Mafia lawyer, a guy who can walk into the room and cast reasonable doubt in the judge's mind. A nut job like Javier Bardem or that other one, what's his name, Tommy Lee something. Not a dancing boy with ballerina shoes."

Patrick gets up, turns around, notes that the pebbles are standard issue, activates the flush mechanism, and, in an avalanche of water, sends the twin stones into the common cesspool.

Sitting on the edge of my bed, I try and think of something else, and forget these invasions of privacy imposed on us, which Patrick seems quite used to. I try and tell myself that all this will pass. At the next interview, I will give simple answers to complex questions, and with the false naivety of a seasoned Pharisee, I will deliver my best *Confiteor*.

In the meantime, I watch Patrick place his little white tablecloth over the toilet bowl. I wish I could get used to it. I can't. It's impossible, despite how often I have seen it.

There is still action in the corridors. I make out the tumult of conflict, angry shouts, insults, then calm returns. Night time and benzodiazepines, widely distributed, begin to do their work. Soon the belly of the prison will start in with its slow digestion, and slowly, too, the men who live in it will disappear, for this short night, into their shared oubliettes.

Doubt and the Pastor

I N 1968, INFLUENCED, I suppose, by the general climate of insurrection, my father bought a strange automobile fitted out with a completely revolutionary motor, elected "car of the year" with great fanfare. The NSU Ro 80 – "Ro" meaning *Rotationskolben* – was a family sedan powered by the famous Comotor block, the first Wankel rotary engine to be used in assembly-line production. The pastor was sensitive to mechanical innovation, and he bought the German four-door model to accommodate a family he could have easily fit into a much more modest space with more conventional technology. Perhaps Johanes still had hopes of expanding his descendants and implanting the Hansen name more solidly in this part of southern France. Whatever the reason, despite its surprising interior comfort, the rotary NSU turned out to be a complete disaster, with a wide array of breakdowns both unexpected and varied. The Ro 80, which was supposed to prefigure the technologies and inventiveness of tomorrow, pared back its ambitions as sales collapsed and soon cast the company single-handedly into bankruptcy. The NSU disappeared, and was finally bought up by Audi. Whatever the case, this vehicle's arrival in our family, a car as celebrated as it was misbegotten, coincided with the deterioration of relations between my father and his wife. And also between the pastor and his church.

During the spring of 1968, the Spargo, whose facade had been freshened up with a quick coat of paint, enjoyed the tonic of those effervescent days. Like all social institutions, the little world of the cinema felt the same libertarian winds of change that were blowing through the factories, universities and avenues of the old world still paved with cobblestones. When she heard Godard in Cannes preaching the celluloid strike and the unification of all struggles, my mother Anna Margerit changed into an Egeria of local repertory, joining the Godard-style tendency, revamping her programme, opening the cavern of the Spargo to all sorts of general assemblies and organising debates about this and that. They were all good as long as they ended late in the night, in the fug of a smoky humid night buzzing with stimulating critiques.

In the afternoon, Anna screened the year's current films, such as *Rosemary's Baby*, *The Party*, *2001: A Space Odyssey* and *Stolen Kisses*. But when evening fell, Marx, Lenin, Trotsky, Mao and Bakunin were the stars of the show, and meetings followed one after the other, waves of small cells that electrified the room in their efforts to prove their respective abilities to "bring class consciousness to the masses".

Sometimes my mother would bring me to these meetings. At the age of thirteen, I discovered unknown territory, and was fascinated by this new language of freedom I had never heard before, a language made of insolence, fury, disrespect and humour, that constantly bombarded life with formulas to raise the dead. Of course, I understood almost nothing of what was being said or played out, but I sensed the original vibration of its meaning, its primary frequency, a sort of "Carle our most noble Emperor and King, Hath tarried now full seven years in Spain". Those words whirled around in my head the way, perhaps, they had turned circles in my grandparents' brains after the roof was wrenched off their Citroën DS 19.

In the lobby of the movie house, Anna taped up large posters with the schedules for each film, the themes of the discussions that would follow, a mishmash of contradictory slogans and information: "How to make a Molotov cocktail. One bottle, two-thirds filled with gasoline, one-third sand, soap powder, a gasoline-soaked rag stuck in the neck." There were magical formulas as well, inexplicably familiar, that made their way into our hearts and immediately found a home. "Press your face against the glass, with the insects." I never forgot that one. Or this one either: "We don't want a world where we're guaranteed not to die of hunger, as we die of boredom." On a large writing desk, the audience could take in warnings with more specific targets, dazibao such as "Godard, the biggest pro-Chinese Swiss asshole" that set off excellent skirmishes in the lobby and on the pavement between Communists who were reputed to be revisionists and ideologically squeaky-clean Maoists, the offspring of bourgeois families. And then there was that standard-size sheet of paper, the most discreet of all, thumbtacked onto the left corner of the least visible of the panels, and when he saw it, one evening when he had come to pick up my mother and me, my father stopped short like a Hungarian pointer in front of his prey, for there was written, "How can a person think freely with a chapel looming over?"

In front of this humble enquiry, the father and husband disappeared in a puff of smoke, and the offended, humiliated churchman, considering himself betrayed by his family, took to the wheel of his Ro 80 equipped with that subtle rotary engine invented by Felix Heinrich Wankel (1902–1988), and escorted his small irresponsible flock back to the apartment on the banks of the river.

I remember everything that took place that night, the words each spoke to challenge the other's certainties, the volume of the voices used to accomplish that task, but also the stifling humidity, the smell of silt rising up from the river, and the chilling sound of the front door when my father slammed it. That night, the man of Skagen left the apartment late in the wee hours, and fled into the shifting sands of his anger.

But before heading for the exit, the pastor threw himself into the furnace of God's wrath. In his scholarly French, seasoned with a pinch of Jutland, he asked, "Don't you understand that you're still married to a pastor? Whether you like it or not, that is your reality. And I remind you, in view of your position, that you are obliged to show some discretion and not insult my ministry. I did not like it, but I accepted the fact that you never set foot in my church. Most of my faithful think I am not even married. I said nothing when you told me you were opening your movie theatre to hold political meetings, most of which end in fistfights broken up by the police. And neither did I say a word when the local newspaper portrayed you as the Pasionaria of the movement and your theatre as 'one of the artistic crucibles of the revolutionary avant-garde'. But this evening, when I read 'How can a person think freely with a chapel looming over?' stuck on one of your corkboards, in your theatre, I felt truly ashamed and humiliated. I can't understand, I really can't. And how can you bring along your thirteen-year-old son to watch goings-on like that, and listen to insurgent students trotting out their idiot theories and insulting each other? What is a boy that age doing, at night, in a place like that? Is that normal? I don't know what you want, Anna, I don't understand you anymore."

As intense as the Red Army at Stalingrad, my mother's counter-attack rained down on the poor pastor. Anna's argument took up the essential points of the new warriors who were fighting to take back control over their lives, and free themselves from their gods and masters, return power to the people who toiled in the factories, and, why not, at the end of history, live lives of unbridled pleasure.

For a pastor of the times, be he a Dane from Skagen, the son of fisherfolk from a long line thereof, nourished on plaice and smoked eel, raised in an atmosphere of tolerance and respect, the message was violent, sudden and hard to choke down in one swallow.

Which is why, that night, Johanes Hansen broke off the exchange, slammed our front door, rushed down the stone staircase, got into his car, which issued its characteristic motor noise, and drove away from his family under the plane trees of the quai Lombard.

Unable, deep down, to separate the threads of good and evil, and predict what the future world's credo would be; unable, that night, to locate the slightest spark of faith in his heart.

This afternoon, the walk in the exercise yard did not last long. At minus twenty, very few of us were willing to go out for a breath of fresh air. Patrick and I were the exceptions to the rule, though I could scarcely stand the cold that seared my air passages and turned my extremities to ice. He, on the other hand, seemed to be made of some isothermal material that insulated him from winter. At even colder temperatures, lying on the bench, I watched him do his workout routine in the yard, bare-armed, as if he were pumping springtime iron. That was how he liked to mark his alpha male territory, displaying his impressive physique and keeping guards and other prisoners at a distance, most of whom, in a confrontation, understood only the primal alphabet and language of intimidation.

Today, for the first time, he talked about his father, who taught mechanical engineering in a college. A man who never took vacation or time off, always busy with his teaching, dedicated to preparing the hundreds of teenagers for the trades of tomorrow and, according to Patrick, completely forgetting about his wife and three children, whom he ignored when he came across them in his house. "At first, when we were kids, me and my brother and sister, we wondered if we'd done something wrong to make him treat us that way. In the end, we went and asked our mother. She gave us the absolutely stupidest answer of all the possible stupid answers. 'He has a lot of work.' We got the picture. Our mother didn't want to talk about it. So we did what he did, we lived off to one side and acted like he wasn't there. One day, just to be sure, I went and hid outside the college to see what my father was like with other people. And fuck me, between two classes, I saw a completely different person. He looked young and alive, he was talking to everyone, making jokes with the asshole students, smiling and looking at them like they were his own kids. And the worst thing is that he really seemed to love them, really, he spoke more to them in the break between two classes than he had to us in our whole lives. I swear, that day, I cried. I didn't say anything about it to my brother and sister. We went on living in that weird way and, as soon as I could, I left home. Today, the bastard is retired. My mother is still with him. I call her once in a while. We never mention his name. It's like he's dead."

We went and sat down on the big bench bolted into the cement yard. We kept our silence. The icy wind whipped our faces and slipped through our tuques. Evening was slowly falling and soon this spot would be as dark as the tomb. A prisoner I had never seen before came and sat on the other end of the bench. Before he could get comfortable, without glancing in his direction, Patrick told him, "Get lost." The guy jumped up like he had been shocked with a cattle prod and hurried away like a man who had seen the abyss open up before him.

When we got back to our cell, we found two guards ransacking the place and searching every possible spot. The toilet towel was on a mattress, a handful of T-shirts had been thrown in front of the crapper, toothpaste and toothbrushes were scattered on the floor. "Fuck, what the hell are you Siamese twins doing here?" Complete search. Drugs had been found in our sector. As the guards were leaving, Patrick motioned them over. "Shit, you'll never find anything. I hid it all here." And just in case they did not catch on, Patrick grabbed his cock and balls through his pants and hustled them as the guards looked on. Neither Siamese twin was moved to check whether his allegations were well founded. Seeing he had won the fight, he did not hold back. "There's a real load in there, and it's top-quality stuff."

When the door slid shut, we had to put everything back where it was, fold up our clothes, and clean what had been dirtied. Patrick raged on like a caged gorilla, separated from his tribe and mistreated by his captors. When everything was tidy, he opened his sketchbook, took out his pencils, and, spontaneously, drew a number of straight lines, and others that were broken, regular curves and approximate shapes. Like a disciple of the Skagen school, he disappeared silently into the universe of perfect light, the peninsula where fathers never existed, a place known to him alone where, since he could not remake the world, he had spent his life ever since childhood trying to remember what it looked like.

It took some time to reduce the fault line that May '68 drew across my parents' lives. At age thirty-eight, my mother threw herself headlong into History's crucible, while on the other side of the glass, my father, hands clasped behind his back, had no choice but to watch her burn.

During the year that followed the events, my parents worked to repair the damage that the bombardment of liberation had inflicted on their marriage. In the summer of 1969, the whole family, meticulously seated on the grey velvet seats of the NSU Ro 80, set out to cover the 2,420 kilometres separating two planets that belonged to radically different solar systems. Against all odds, the bi-rotor displayed its best side, and ate up the distance in a little over two days, Anna and Johanes spelling each other off at the wheel. It was my first time in Jutland. When I arrived, whipped by the winds that sculpted the dunes, basking in that diaphanous light that set a silvery haze upon the surface of the water, surrounded by a benevolent family the size of a small army, I had the strange feeling that I was finally living among my people. Soon, like them, I would be speaking to the herring, deciphering the storms, and, flanked by two Hansens, by the warehouse silos, I, too, would be bagging fishmeal to feed other fish.

Everyone spoke in lusty voices, and their laughter rang out like church bells in the four corners of the great room where we gathered. All manner of food was set out on small plates, and these hungry giants made short work of the provisions. My mother and I did not understand much of what was being said, but we grasped our glasses firmly in our hands and did our best to keep prescribed smiles on our lips, like a pair of British tourists on vacation, timid intruders hoping to drop anchor. From time to time, my father would turn to us, take us by the waist, and introduce us to another Hansen, even bigger than the one before, who would explode in laughter as he listened to Johanes deliver an anecdote that concerned us but that we did not understand. Then, little by little, the room emptied of its population, which gathered, men and women together, in the yard. In another century, they would have come together around a team of Friesians, but today they made a circle around the Ro 80. My father lifted the bonnet and revealed to his family the secrets of the Wankel rotary engine, which functioned according to the Otto cycle. The Hansens listened to my father's explanations in respectful silence, not at all unnerved by the turbulent winds whistling discreetly over the crest of the roof. The family was like an assembly of the faithful captivated by a car mechanic's sermon telling of the patient and divine construction of a perfect world.

I understood early on that the Protestant church was not a demanding sport. Its rules were relaxed, and free of the rigid framework and liturgical yoke of Catholicism. Every parish could organise its services as it wished, nothing was centralised, and the pastors held no real power. Essentially, they commented on religious texts or called upon outside speakers to liven up their weekly encounters. And so, the Sunday after our arrival, my father was invited by Henrik Glass, the pastor of Skagen, to stand before the microphone and lead the assembly in the direction he saw fit. According to the résumé he supplied afterwards, Johanes began by evoking the dance of the sand pushed by winds that came from every corner of the world, the squalls of novelty and temptation eroding our lives, insidiously covering over our churches and our faith. He evoked the tumult breaking over our lives, the legitimate doubts and questioning that the times might well create in our hearts; he ground his way through a number of other metaphors I have since forgotten, then concluded with his favourite tune, the chapel buried in sand and the duty we had, all through our lives, to dig and push away the sands, that we might continue, together, every Sunday, to be united within our faith.

His words seemed to make a big impression on the locals. On the parvis, they gathered around my father to thank him and congratulate him on his remarkable sermon. The warm reception made my father blush with pleasure, especially since the texts he worked so hard to write ended up lost in the indifference of his listeners back in Toulouse.

My mother and I knew the business about the sands by heart, and we stood to one side there in the state of Denmark. We waited patiently for the fervour of the faithful to drain away, after which we would sit down to family lunch with the Jutland ogres.

As we were set to leave, and already sitting in the Ro 80, a man came running up to my father's open window. They conversed a minute, and I saw Johanes display his most charming smile. He stepped out of the car and opened its generous bonnet. There followed a long conversation concerning the comparative virtues of the Wankel engine. His partner in conversation – later we would learn he was about to acquire this collection of woes – listened religiously to his pastor's word, who was quick to bear witness to his faith in this audacious mechanical advancement. That day, it excited him more than divine extravagance.

During the stay in Jutland, at my age of embarrassment, I realised how much Danish men enjoyed looking at my mother. Wherever we went, I saw that her look, her shape and the beauty of her features captured their attention. It is not easy for a boy of fourteen to accept that his mother is sexy, and through the power of that one word, understand that she is a woman who has escaped the world of his childhood, broken out of his register, she incarnates someone different whom he no longer recognises and who holds the strange power, even while being the pastor's wife, to excite men's desire, because she possesses that divine something, those attributes, that magic sum, those secret forms that every man on earth dreams of. She was thirty-nine years old, and my mother, but I would have to learn who this new woman was, for she would be living with us every day, in our house.

The Danish stay was a formidable elixir for each of us. My father recovered the smells of his native land, the uproar of his two seas and the warmth of his family. My mother opened herself to the luminous beauty of the landscapes. As for me, I learned a few essential phrases, *Mange tak!* (Thank you very much!), *Jeg er ikke sulten længere* (I'm not hungry anymore), *Je her søven* (I'm sleepy), *Eller er min far?* (Where is my father?) and *Der ere en smuk båd!* (That's a nice boat!). I also learned, despite my French education, the lessons of my teachers, and my mother tongue, that I was, above all, a Hansen. There was something undefinable in me that came from this place and would always draw me back. Who knows why, but at the age of fourteen I took it into my head that one day, when the time was right, I would return to die in the land of the giants.

The trip home was nothing like the carefree jaunt that had led us to the far tip of the peninsula. The first breakdown occurred in Aarhus. A long whistling noise, bucking and the motor decided to take a three-hour break. A relay switch in the semi-automatic gearbox. A local mechanic put things back in order until the fuel pump stalled us in Hamburg overnight. The next morning, with a new part, we headed towards Dortmund, where the neighbourhood NSU dealer watched as we were towed into his garage. We emerged from it mid-afternoon the next day without ever knowing the reason behind the breakdown. The German technician tried his best to explain in English the origin of the failure of an element that was hidden, so it seemed, somewhere underneath the cylinder head. The good man kept repeating "chatter marks" and "rotor housing" and pointing his index finger emphatically at the upper part of the engine, but neither my mother nor my father understood what was lurking behind his grumbling and sign language. Running out of arguments, the mechanic used a universal word common to German, Danish and French: guarantee. Then he added, several times, *Kein Geld, nein, kein Geld.* Which means, if you were to elaborate, "You bought a useless piece of shit, and NSU, which knows it better than anyone, will still respect the guarantee and pay for your repairs. You owe me nothing. *Nein.*"

We covered the remaining thousand kilometres in one shot, the way you might swallow a bitter potion. Paris by night, the RN 20, Étampes, Orléans, Châteauroux, Limoges, Brive, Cahors and, at daybreak, in the glow of rosy dawn, the slow descent towards the plains of the Garonne.

Turning off the ignition, after he parked close to the quai Lombard, my father ran his hand over his face. "What a strange trip." My mother opened her window and gazed at the river. Despite the early hour and the impediments of the difficult trip, neither of them seemed in any hurry to exit the car and return to their ordinary lives. Perhaps they preferred to prolong the feeling of togetherness that had united them through the interminable trip back, spelling each other off at the wheel to reach a common goal, which was to arrive at their apartment door, though each secretly dreaded that, sooner or later, it would slam shut once more.

"Chatter marks," said my father. "Rotor housing," my mother answered, smiling. Then they stepped out of the Ro 80.

I received a message from my evaluator this morning. He wanted to know if I would agree to participate in a self-expression workshop run by a psychologist, during which each participant would describe his "life journey" to the others, and the reasons that led him to Bordeaux Prison. If I understood correctly, the session would follow the model of Alcoholics Anonymous. "Hello, my name is John, and I'm here for aggravated assault. I haven't hit anyone in eight months." A chorus of "Great, John, good work!" would follow, and then applause.

I decided not to answer Viggo Mortensen. I'd had a different idea of the man, and I was disappointed.

"Shit, when you read crap like that, it really freaks you out.

You ever read the Bible? Hey, I'm talking to you about the Bible." That's the last question I expected to hear from Patrick Horton. No, I, the pastor's son, have never read the Bible. But how did he get his hands on one? "My mother crammed it into my bag just as I was leaving for this place. 'It can't do any harm,' she told me. Shit, I opened this thing ten minutes ago and believe me, those guys were radical, when they decided something, there was no looking back. Our judges would handle them with kid gloves. Listen to this. Before the text I'll give you the name of the guy who wrote it and a number that goes with it that doesn't make any sense to me. Isaiah 65:12: 'Therefore will I number you to the sword, and ye shall all bow down to the slaughter: because when I called, ye did not answer; when I spake, ye did not hear; but did evil before mine eyes, and did choose that wherein I delighted not.' Really, the guy is hardcore. He sure don't mess around! Wait, listen to this one, Matthew 25:30: 'And cast ye the unprofitable servant into outer darkness: there shall be weeping and gnashing of teeth.' Bang, crash, the end! And last but not least, Leviticus 20:15: 'And if a man lie with a beast, he shall surely be put to death: and ye shall slay the beast.' No shit, those guys were as crazy as cockroaches. Slay the beast – the poor animal had nothing to do with any of it."

Then the Bible performed a majestic flying leap across our cell. Like a bird brought down by shot, it crashed against the foot of the wall stained with saltpetre, behind which the scratching of rodents could be heard.

. . .

In the middle of the night, Patrick Horton gave a scream so heart-rending and powerful that it threw me out of bed, and had the two guards, the Siamese twins, charging in, tasers and billyclubs in hand, to put an end to what they thought was a violent assault. "I saw it, it was right there, it was walking on my stomach and staring at me. I don't know if it was a big mouse or a rat, but fuck, that thing was walking right on me. I saw it, chief, I saw it. You've got to change my cell, I can't stay here. I can't stand rodents, really, they make me sick. You've got to do something, shit, call the warden, call whoever you want to, but do something." The guards were fascinated by the collapse of a myth, the fall of a gang boss, but still, they tried to explain that they could not wake up the warden for a mouse. The prison was one big rat trap where all sorts of vermin have been swarming since the beginning of its existence. Everybody knew that. And since everyone knew that, they were not going to summon the head cheese over a rodent.

Vengeance is mine; I will repay, saith the Bible. The Siamese twins sat down and provided a detailed explanation of the situation to Patrick, the feared Hell's Angels hitman. At two o'clock in the morning, they were still speaking to him in the same gentle tones, with the reasoned empathy mothers use when they try to calm their children who stand terrified at the gates of a dreadful nightmare in the middle of the night. "I can't. I don't give a shit, I just can't. Get me out of here. If you don't have another cell, lock me up in the infirmary. I'm not joking, I'm going to lose my mind. Fuck, rats, I can't stand it. Come on, take me to the infirmary."

As incredible as it sounds, the guards radioed the guy on

duty at the medical facility, then they nodded to Patrick. Like a kid who has just had some enormous punishment lifted, he threw on a sweater and pants, and, without a backwards glance for Isaiah, Matthew or even me, he shot out of the cell like a man with the devil on his tail.

The Depth of their Throats

I UNDERSTOOD VERY EARLY on that my father would never be a true Frenchman, one of those guys who was convinced England has always been a place of perdition, and that the rest of the world is a distant suburb lacking in refinement.

The difficulty he had in living in France and understanding the country, endorsing its customs and habits, displeased my mother so much that their recurring conversations on the subject often awoke other points of discord. In spite of the sixteen years he had spent here, Johanes Hansen was a Dane to the core. An eater of *smørrebrød*, a man from North Jutland, unbending when it came to keeping his word, looking straight in the eye of the man standing before him, free of that excitable dialectic in vogue among people here who were so quick to deny the obvious and disavow commitment.

Of the country that took him in, above all he loved its language, and used it with infinite respect and the greatest grammatical accuracy. As for the rest, he seemed to have a hard time finding a life that suited him. He often said that of all the nations he knew, France was the country that had the most difficulty applying the moral, republican virtues it demanded of others. Especially when it came to equality and fraternity. "With their crowns of privilege, your presidents and little marquis look much more like royalty than our poor Queen Margrethe II." He would often say that at table to spur my mother on. He could not tolerate the arrogance, the easy lies and the disloyalty he claimed flowed down from our governments like water. Our politicians? He described them wading through baths of corruption and compromise.

Anna would cut short his cavalcade of blame. "Why live here? You're free to return." My father never answered back, but all of us heard the sound of his sweet voice. "My son is here, and I love you."

I was born and educated in France, but I shared most of my father's negative views and feelings about the country. I fully understood that a man of his stature, raised in the tides of pacifism and internationalism, felt cramped in the French straitjacket into which he was supposed to fit. But his son was there, and even though it was becoming more complicated, he continued to love his wife.

The Spargo went back to its calm existence and the ebb and flow that followed the releases of successful films. In 1970, *Le Cercle Rouge*, *Tristana*, *Little Big Man*, *Le Boucher*, *M*A*S*H* and *The Confession* gave my mother one of her best years. The output was generous, with brilliant new movies that fit perfectly into our repertory niche, where the people in the know wanted to be seen. In high school, I was popular thanks to my mother's position and the incredible film fever that burned among youth in those days.

I saw every Spargo movie, one after the other. Sometimes, depending on the day, most often at the end of the morning and for a special occasion, a landmark film, my mother would organise a family screening. We would have the theatre to ourselves. Sitting side by side, my father, mother and I would watch a feature on the big screen. It was an unforgettable experience. As the images from those cellulose triacetate reels flowed past, in this giant living room, we were the very picture of a close-knit family.

My father told us almost nothing about his church and what he was doing there. His Danish performances had been crowned by ardent encores, but here he seemed to provide only minimal service in the face of polite indifference. He always wrote his sermons diligently, but something in him had been dampened down. My mother never attended a service, and I had long since stopped going to listen to his nonsense, which, like that of his colleagues and competitors, had been turning circles for centuries on the turntable of the prophets.

Some evenings, as he waited for my mother, Johanes would pour himself a drink and sit in front of the big window facing the river. In the summer, when it rained, he would open the panels wide to listen to the sound of the rain and take in the wet smell of life rising up from the pavement. Coming from a man of the church, with his melancholy and sometimes disillusioned faith, you might think he would have chosen Bach or Handel to embellish those solitary evenings. But in his moments of disenchantment, my father would listen to recordings that seemed to have fallen off the shelf in no particular order: Lee Konitz, Emerson, Lake & Palmer,

Stan Getz, Curtis Mayfield and Led Zeppelin would parade past on our Marantz hi-fi system connected to JBL speakers personally chosen by my mother. Sound was of paramount importance in my parents' time, though it is no longer so today. There was astonishing competition to purify the imperfections of pressing, botched production and the sputtering of 33s ploughed by rivers of diamonds. For the pastor, this music was heaven-sent, and he owed it to the impenetrable channels of tweeters, midranges and woofers designed by James Bullough Lansing (JBL) and assembled in Northridge, California.

If Johanes were still of this world, and had he read the account of the misfortunes of my small life, at least he would have been satisfied to hear this useless but precise note about the origin of our loudspeakers. "Today, the world has become too complex to settle for approximations, fuzzy explanations and vague remarks. More than ever, I believe we must strive for correctness, accuracy, naming the detail. In the past, you could buy a man's soul with a pious image and in return give no more than a blessing. Today, to obtain what I have come to ask, you will have to accompany the brother, answer his questions, calm his fears, and tuck him in with all the patience of a tired recruiter from Alcoholics Anonymous."

Thus spake my father. When he finished his first or second drink, facing the rain, he would sometimes describe his pet enterprise, the hours "spent in the perfection of faith". One evening when my mother was late coming up our staircase, perhaps this time after a third glass, with the rain still washing the windows of the apartment, he abruptly let go of the cliff he had been hanging on to for so long. "I have no more faith. Not even enough to fill a day. Not even a few hours here and there. Perfection is no longer an issue; there is nothing left. When we went to Skagen last time, I had a long talk with the old pastor there about these matters. After a time he said to me, 'But Johanes, I have nothing left either, nothing at all, except this bottle of Scotch I will replenish when it is empty. Faith is fragile. It is based on nothing at all, like a magic trick, and what does it take to be a good magician? A rabbit and a hat. There was a time when I had both in the palm of my hand. Today, no more rabbit, no more hat, no more magic.' That's how it is, son. Nothing left. You and your mother are right not to come and see me, and never to have cared about any of this. I envy you. But to make a living, I have to keep going on stage and doing my old trick, the only one I ever learned. And with no wife, no rabbit, no hat."

My father made us aubergine parmigiana for dinner that night. It was waiting in the warm oven. When my mother returned home, she carefully avoided slamming the front door. Johanes had fallen asleep.

At dawn, as if nothing had happened the previous night, Patrick Horton tiptoed back to our cell. Later, as we were returning from breakfast, a guard stuck his head through the half-open door. "I told the chief about your problem. It's all taken care of. A maintenance man will be here in an hour." Around noon, an employee entered our condo with a pointing trowel, metal shavings and a bag of quick-set cement. He diluted the powder in a little water, added the steel shavings, and began filling the cracks in the walls. As he worked, Patrick followed him like a slavish shadow, checking the effectiveness of the repair job. "Are you sure there's enough metal in the mix? Is it sharp enough? They've got to cut their paws, otherwise it's no use. How long before it really hardens? Twenty-four hours? Fuck, isn't there any way to speed it up?" The prison employee spent an hour in our condo, scraping and refilling. He had to get another bag of cement and more metal shards. When he finished, he washed his hands in our sink, looked at the towel on the toilet bowl, and gave us the once-over. "Which one of you is afraid of mice?" It took Patrick a while, but he confessed. The guy put his things away and smiled. "Damn, I knew it all along."

This January has been one of the coldest in Montreal. The temperature dropped to minus thirty-two. In the cells, despite the heating, it does not get any warmer than fourteen degrees. We were given extra blankets. They are acrylic and give off a strange smell like the kind of rubber that is made in China from old, recycled, chopped-up tyres. We sleep with our clothes on, and during the day we put on two or three sweaters to ward off the cold.

Frozen in the bowels of the prison and cut off from their usual routes, the rats and mice have not come back for a return visit. This has had a clear effect on Patrick's mood. He has recovered his splendour, and his desire to kick the ass of a good portion of humanity. "I know one of the guys that came in today. He's a real double-crosser. But there's no-one faster than him in Montreal when it comes to chopping stolen bikes.

He'll do one for you in an afternoon. But don't forget. When you see what he wants from you, you'll understand the guy doesn't work for the Salvation Army. Besides, he's a creep that never goes out without a blade. By the time tomorrow rolls around, he'll have one here. I don't need a crystal ball, I know it's going to end badly for him. One day, I'm telling you, he's going to run into a katana ace who'll cut him to ribbons. Like the Good Book says, He who threatens you with a dagger will end up in the meat grinder." On that note, my favourite exegete wrapped himself in his blanket and began his guard duties, making sure the vermin entrances were tightly sealed with the souls of sharpened metal.

Whatever the temperature, the food they serve is terrible. Today we had brown chicken fillets with frozen peas partially thawed in the microwave. At these times of culinary depression – in prison, meals are one of the most important events of the day – I do not long for my mother's cooking, for she never used fresh products, but I do dream of the tasty Skagen plaice prepared by my grandfather Sven, who served it with cranberries that combined the essences of sweetness and salt on the palate.

Tonight, it is so cold I can't sleep. I listen to pipes creaking and men coughing. Sometimes the sound of someone's coughing fit reaches me from a cell on another floor. The noise is distorted and muffled by distance, and reminds me of the cries and moaning of a wild animal.

My father stopped by earlier. We talked of this and that and he skilfully slipped the Ro 80 into the thread of our conversation. He was wondering what had become of the car after he left Toulouse at the end of 1975. I knew the answer, but preferred to keep it to myself. It would have disappointed him. Winona and Nouk joined us a little later. It was a moment of peace. We lingered a while, the dead and the living huddled together, hoping to bring one other what we sorely lacked, a little warmth and comfort.

Imprisonment gives off an unpleasant smell. Remnants of macerating evil thoughts, the effluvia of dirty ideas that have been hanging around too long, the bitter whiff of old regrets. Fresh air, by definition, never enters here. We breathe in our own breath in this bell jar, we share the atmosphere shot through with shards of brown chicken and dark intentions. Our clothes, our sheets and our skin end up saturated with these fumes, and there is no getting used to them. When we return from the exercise yard, and the outside air is halted at the turnstiles, the transition is always sudden, and the vague nausea is there to remind us that we live and breathe in a belly pushing us along in its laborious digestion, and then, when the time comes, it will expel us to free itself, not to give us back our freedom.

Earning my *bac* after Lycée at the age of eighteen was not without its challenges. A large number of students drowned, but I was saved from the waters and plucked out by the benevolent hand of chance. Far from the generosity of May '68, when everyone received their diploma simply by presenting a certificate of residency, the Academy of Toulouse, during the years that followed, raised its requirements and standards of acceptance appreciably. My aptitude in sports and geography, as well as a little resourcefulness in other subjects, allowed me to present my final diploma to the pastor and hear him say, in the language of Hans Christian Andersen, with a certain solemnity, "*Min søn, jeg er stolt af dig*," which accurately translates as, "My son, I am proud of you."

The truth is, I never really knew whether the half-blond mixture I sometimes felt I was in my father's eyes made him regret not having married a real Skagen woman, who would have thought Danish, loved Danish, eaten Danish, swum Danish, fucked Danish and given birth to a robust Danish baby whose strength and beauty would have been praised by all, but who, as soon as he opened his eyes, would have whispered to his close admirers, *Smigger er som en skygge: det gor du, eller større, eller mindre.* Flattery is like a shadow: it doesn't make you bigger or smaller.

I would have understood it perfectly well if Johanes, the pastor who spoke the Law without faith, had dreamed of the little branch he never had as he watched the rain on those long evenings.

The university welcomed me as a supernumerary immigrant, and the geography department thought it right to teach me that Denmark, with its 42,924 square kilometres, was the smallest country in Scandinavia. That is, as long as we neglected its satellites, Greenland and the Faroe Islands, which belonged to it, turning it into a mastodon weighing in at 2,210,579 square kilometres.

I loved the geography of travel, the geography that you journey across on foot, on a human scale, educated by slopes and inclines, the fatigue of your legs and the whims of the heavens. I was much less taken by the books illuminated by graphs and data. My stay on the campus was a series of casual comings and goings, tests of my misunderstanding, photocopied handouts interspersed with endless days at the cinema, which, when evening came, returned me to my family, enlightened but with stiff limbs.

At home, things went on as usual, eroding the patience of one partner and the love of the other a little more each day. The apartment on the quai Lombard was filled with that atmosphere, and the signs of indifference settled like layers of dust. The pastor continued to prepare the meals and my mother continued to come home late. Most of the time, they dined on their own, keeping different schedules.

Anna kept track of her business revenue, worked on her programming and took casual advantage of the world as it presented itself. Johanes tried to maintain his position, writing in silence about the word of God, tinkering with the appearance of illusions, improvising a small magic trick with what he had at hand, though without the slightest hat or the tiniest rabbit.

The year 1975, when I turned twenty, marked the end of a world, ours, the world of the Hansens, those from the North and the South, who had travelled so many kilometres and made so many intimate sacrifices to unite, learn unknown languages, buy unlikely vehicles, fuck however they could, one closing his eyes, the other not, make a child without knowing for whom or why, preach God's word, programme the devil's deeds, and, as they had been made to promise, each day sweep away the sands that accumulated before their door, enduring all those things to the point of exhaustion, only to end up separated, detached, disjointed, torn and broken.

On April 24 of that year, just before noon, a victim of the bad taste in automotive fashion, but also of age and, most of all, the sudden shock of oil prices, the last DS model left the Citroën factories on the quai de Javel. It was an industrial funeral, a ceremony that drew few tears. Present or represented were company and government officials, press officers and, no doubt, my grandparents, standing somewhere in the factory where this car was produced and, before it, large quantities of poisonous sodium hypochlorite. The Margerits made a point of being present at that funeral to witness the disappearance of the last representative of what they considered to be a long line of murderers. They had not forgotten, let alone forgiven, the accident at Naurouze.

Later, when I thought back to the liquidation of the Hansen family, though I could not draw a complete analogy, I always associated it with the Citroën bankruptcy. The sale of their brand. Their exodus from the former bleach factory.

We left the quai Lombard and the directory of good families largely because of a certain Gerardo Rocco Damiano. This Bronx native and devout Catholic, a former assistant in a radiology clinic who later became a neighbourhood hairdresser, raised twenty-five thousand dollars from benefactors from the parishes of organised crime, and set out to make the second true pornographic film produced by the professional American film industry. The script and dialogue were lighter than air, the story was based exclusively on the oral-pharyngeal extravagances of the heroine, Linda Lovelace, backed up by amateur actors ready to give generously of themselves. The shoot, put together with a crew housed in a VW Beetle, was wrapped in six days during the mild Miami winter. When the film was released in the United States in spring 1972, one of the stars, Harry Reems, who until then had played only Shakespeare, worked on *Deep Throat* as a lighting designer as well. He later found himself the object of prosecution for "conspiring to transport obscene material across state lines". The film was banned in twenty-seven states, was described as "totally obscene" by a New York judge and set off storms of scandal, volleys of criticism and dizzying displays of virtue. Those theatres where screenings were permitted overflowed with spectators. During its career, *Deep Throat*, a low-budget wonder, brought in more than 600 million dollars. But Damiano, the hairdresser–director, along with the apprentice actors, received only dust from this mountain of gold for their six days of work. The vast majority of the receipts were collected, in cash, on a daily basis, at the ticket offices of theatres across the country by a garrison of collection agents charged by the Mafia with fleecing the actors and the hairdresser.

Undeterred, Gerardo Damiano did it again the next year, shooting *The Devil in Miss Jones*, which generated a box office of 7.7 million and was the biggest hit of 1973. In a career spanning thirty-two years, the filmography of this astonishing personage came to a halt after forty-eight pictures whose wonderfully explicit titles, such as *Splendor in the Ass* (1989), leave no doubt as to the writing, nature and content of the screenplays.

I remember these details because, held back by the barbed wire of censorship, *Deep Throat* was not released in France until August 27, 1975. During that long period of waiting, the debate between Reformation and Repertory raged in our house.

Three years had passed since the American screening. Three years during which ENT doctors and critics theorised about the singularities of this very deep throat, its director's biography, his elastic Catholicism and the profits that disappeared like so many rabbits into Sicilian hats. The anecdotes arrived in waves from the far side of the Atlantic, so when *Deep Throat* was finally shown in our theatres, everyone felt they had already seen the film.

The date of August 27, 1975 is unforgettable, the fateful day when our lives were turned upside down, making official what I had sensed for some time.

As early as June, the Minister of Culture, Michel Guy, lifted the ban blocking the arrival of these celluloid reels. My mother, as an independent exhibitor, negotiated with the distributor Alpha France to present the phenomenon at the Spargo. The news, when it reached the quai Lombard, enraged the pastor, revealing his prudish, conservative side, yet loosening his tongue. "Do you really think I give a shit about that miserable business, your ridiculous clitoris and those guys who get sucked for an hour? You think that's what shocks me? You really think that? No, Anna, what pisses me off is that the pastor's wife didn't consider for one second the repercussions that her bullshit movie choices were going to have on me. If you play this film in your theatre, I'm finished, I won't be able to show my face at church. Everyone – the press, my congregation – is going to make the connection between the person who caused the scandal and the person who, on Sundays, preaches from Corinthians: 'He that committeth fornication sinneth against his own body.' Do you have any idea how much trouble you're going to get me into? And without even discussing it, or asking my opinion. I learned by accident when I picked up the phone. A guy from some outfit called Alpha France says to me, 'Is Mrs Hansen there? Are you Mr Hansen? I have good news. It's a go for *Deep Throat*. You'll be able to show the film as soon as it's available. We'll let you know the date when the reels arrive. I'm warning you, it'll be a change from your usual programming.' If you release this film, my whole life will change, Anna, *our* whole life."

My mother jumped to her feet and banged the table with her open hand. "You're just a small-time pastor from the provinces, a prudish Protestant, conservative and blind to change. You see nothing, you understand nothing, you decide, you judge, you brandish your Bible like the Criminal Code. You're still living in the nineteenth century with your fishmeal and your church in the sand. You piss me off, Johanes Hansen. Everyone, everywhere, is going to see this movie. I'm sure it's a piece of trash, but it's going to be a turning point in my profession. I don't know in which direction it'll go, but I'm sure it's going to be big. So I'm telling you, I'm not going to give all that up to ease the anxieties of a husband who can't accept his wife's work. I show films, Johanes, you know that, it's my job. When I get a Bergman or a Tarkovsky, I show metaphysics and mysticism. When it's a Damiano, I show blowjobs,

blowjobs and clits. I'm terribly sorry if a little thing at the back of a woman's throat can throw you into such a state."

On that note, Anna left the room and slammed the front door hard on the way out of the apartment.

That evening, I understood that my father and I were like the last Citroën DS to roll off the assembly line. Ahead and behind us, an abyss of loneliness and uncertainty. In the family conflict, though I obviously shared my mother's liberal, pragmatic, modern point of view, I immediately sided with Johanes. No doubt that was due to a kind of close Danish solidarity, but also I was deeply disturbed by the sight of my helpless father, having lost his faith and forgotten his magic tricks, and been stripped of his language, watching the curtains of rain fall as he waited for my mother. His life moved against the grain of all the films I was seeing, and the world around us. Like the Wankel engine in his NSU, it ran circles without moving forward, not engaging enough to pull out of the rut.

Then what had to happen, happened. A free publication that specialised in shows and upcoming movie releases listed the Spargo as one of the theatres presenting *Deep Throat*. The polemics in the press took off as the release date approached, and certain leagues of virtue fiercely criticised the unnatural use of this particular throat. In the Protestant sphere, where everyone had made the connection between the tumultuous theatre operator and Pastor Hansen, there was increasing difficulty when it came to finding the appropriate response to the insistent questions put forward by the community's less progressive fringe.

On August 22, 1975, a Friday, my father was summoned by the church council. The members explained to him that, because of the rather particular situation that could put everyone in an embarrassing position, they had decided to suspend his position as a precautionary measure, effective immediately.

Back at the apartment, I found a man without a voice, absent from himself.

On Sunday morning, August 24, Johanes stayed home. He walked down to the quay along the Garonne, then made a number of phone calls, including one in English. There was no communication with Denmark. He must have decided to leave his family out of the commotion, and avoid criticising my mother by having to explain his troubles. The previous Friday, after the discussion, my father had known that his dismissal was final, and he would never return to his church. How could he have justified his return, and his continued presence, since Anna's modernity had involved him in programming *The Devil in Miss Jones* the following year and, the year after that, *Splendor in the Ass*?

Needless to say, the August 25 screenings were sold out, as were those over the following days and weeks. Of course, the film was a shoddy piece of work, and a local critic, after watching it, described it as a picture for "visual gluttons".

My father rarely left the quai Lombard. He seemed to have accepted defeat. I noticed he spent a lot of time on the phone, speaking French and English. With my mother, the discussion was closed, and he communicated with her only to settle routine, domestic matters that had to be attended to. Not a word about Damiano or Linda Lovelace. Little by little, the din died down. At first distraught at her husband's sudden disgrace, Anna quickly recovered her shine, got back on her feet and cheerfully began enjoying her success and the revenues that no shady collector would come to claim.

In mid-September, at dinnertime, as a storm raged outside, whipping the plane trees with its cutting winds, my father's calm, composed voice rose above the crash of thunder. "I have two things to tell you," he announced to us. "First, the church council received me last week and confirmed, without going further into the reasons for my dismissal, that I will not be reinstated in my position. The other news is that I have found a new job. I will be appointed Senior Pastor of the Methodist Church in Thetford Mines, a small town in Canada, in the province of Quebec. I will take up my new duties on November 1, and will be moving there in mid-October. Between now and then I will do my best to erase administratively – I know you French are very fond of the sport – all signs of my presence in this town and this family. Considering these conditions, our divorce, Anna, seems to me to be a necessary step. I leave it to you to choose the terms, and of course I will sign before I leave all the documents you will need. Needless to say, both of you will always be welcome in this little town I know nothing about, except that it has grown rich thanks to its asbestos mines."

With the determination of a true Dane from the peninsula, my mother rose from the table and glared insolently and furiously at Johanes Hansen and his watery blue eyes. At that moment, he must have looked like an insignificant pastor to her. "The divorce papers have already been prepared. You will find them in the cupboard drawer in the hall."

"Hey, twit, what are you thinking about?" I did not think Patrick had it in him to ask me the question, or call me "twit" in that friendly way. I could have told him I had been hanging out in a world buried for years now, a distant world where you could divorce over a bad film, a world I had scarcely lived in for twenty years, but where I still had a spot, sitting at the table between my father and mother, who, that evening, were together for one of the very last times. Of that world, there is nothing left today. The pastor died before my eyes. Anna, after living for a while in common-law union with a minor Swiss film producer, had died five years earlier from a voluntary overdose of medication. The NSU, stolen and totally destroyed in a road wreck shortly after my father left, finished its run at a salvager's. As for the Spargo, its destiny followed market trends, and it slowly declined. My mother sold it to a young Marseilles businessman who quickly abandoned the repertory label and transformed the venue into a porno candy store, the Prado, which was then renamed the Zig-Zag, before being replaced by an eyewear franchise that did not exhibit much interest in the property's past.

That was what this twit was thinking about on a January evening as the temperature plummeted. Soon our blankets would not be enough to keep us warm. The boilers, pushed to the limit, were too old to counterbalance winter's excess.

"Did you see what happened yesterday in New York, and

in plenty of other cities? Three thousand guys took off their pants all at the same time. Three thousand in one fell swoop, can you believe it? It was No Pants Day. The announcer said something like 'The members of this club do it to feel liberated without their pants. During the day, they go about their normal lives at work and on the street, but in their underwear.' No kidding, it's like a dream. Can you imagine a guard showing up at our condo in a thong and yelling, 'Hansen to the visiting room!'? Or the judge in the courtroom, in his undies, handing you twenty years? No Pants Day would be fucking hot. I'm telling you, man, we're living in a crazy world. I don't mind if they want to let them jangle free in the fresh air. But in January, with the weather we're having, it's a fucking extreme sport."

Something dark and hard to throw off, a heavy shawl of sadness, fell upon my shoulders. Patrick continued broadcasting the headlines from his new radio culture, but his messages faded out before they could reach me.

I often felt this absence. Always the same unease. When I dug up my dead, so numerous, my solitude spoke its name loud and clear. I was the last of the southern Hansens.

Thetford Mines

AFTER MY FATHER left, Anna made no effort to get closer to me. She went on living her life as if nothing had happened, ostentatiously ignoring the long shadow of the pastor, who still continued to come and go in our apartment. At the time, I was deeply resentful towards my mother for having been so unyielding with Johanes, letting him leave as if he had never been more than a visitor. The break never healed. The following summer, it was my turn to take a plane to Canada, and join my father.

These days, Thetford Mines is still part geological aberration, part aesthetic curiosity. Outside the name, which offers a clue, it is nothing remarkable from a purely factual point of view. The city (45° 6' north and 71° 18' west) has some twenty-five thousand inhabitants spread out, on average, at a density of one hundred per square kilometre, over a modest total surface area of 225.79 square kilometres. The discreet Bécancour River flows through it, and the town lies halfway between

Quebec City to the north and Sherbrooke to the south. It is part of the Chaudière-Appalaches administrative district. It boasts a general hospital, a college, a congress centre and an indoor swimming pool: tokens of relative prosperity. Every year, it organises the Festival Promutuel de la Relève, as well as a parade of antique automobiles. The Assurancia and the Thetford Blue Sox are, respectively, the city's hockey and baseball teams.

When you actually arrive there, this illustrated catalogue of goods and services disappears, and you are confronted by phenomenal excavations that surround the city centre and perforate the earth upon which it stands. This is the world after Armageddon. Mines and more mines, deep strip mines, scouring the belly of the earth, gigantic lunar craters, oversized Martian pits with staircases cut into them, terraces striated with hairpin roads, dusty slag heaps, lurking and curled like enormous sleeping beasts. Here and there stand lakes that seem to have fallen out of the sky, filled with fabulous emerald water, like small seas designed by a jeweller, supernatural and luminescent in this devastated landscape of scars, sadness and greyness.

The name of the last small municipality recently swallowed up by Thetford Mines, Amiante, sums up the nature of the mineral deposits. To make sure everyone understands, the neighbouring town is called Asbestos.

And that was where my father lived, in this cauldron of fibre and dust, this incredible decor of mines, this unreal, bombed-out, slashed-through, dug-up site where, since the year 1876, chrysotile has been king.

The man who launched the operation and discovered the mineral by scraping at the ground with his fingernail went by the name of Joseph Fecteau. He was a farmer with golden fingers. After him, Roger Ward, the Johnson brothers and many others who worked the earth in this new fashion undertook to mine the ground down to its very bones, devastating the landscape, quartering the land and, with the help of explosives, blowing apart heaps of rocks with their load of white asbestos fibre that the geologists of the University of Montreal, specialists in the Quaternary era, described in their writings on "the three stratigraphic sequences that constitute the Pleistocene epoch in the Thetford Mines region".

The pastor preached in the heart of the Paleolithic. He had travelled the world only to return to its origins, the time when the first humans appeared, equipped with carved stones. From the cockpits of steam shovels that could put a scratch on heaven, their descendants dug up the vestiges of their origins, digging away at the accumulations of strata like metal mastiffs eager to recover the bone they buried.

The strip mines usually bear the names of the companies that exploit them, and naturally lend their patronyms to the streets that border the open pits. The companies have names like King, Bell, Beaver, Johnson and so on. The inhabitants' houses hover on the edge of the abyss, great pits where giant dump trucks roam and act as conveyor belts between the centre of the earth, its fibrous entrails, and the surface, where the dusty light of the landscape has never inspired a school of painting.

In 1975, Thetford Mines was one of the world's major sites

for chrysotile, producing the material with neither remorse nor respite. No-one was particularly concerned by the twenty-six health studies published between 1934 and 1954 that related cases of asbestosis and lung cancer among patients working in the asbestos sector in Pennsylvania, Wales and the province of Quebec.

But in Paris, in 1975, the year that my father settled into the belly of Thetford Mines, the asbestos scandal broke at the Jussieu university faculty. It was discovered that this material, present in the buildings, had aged badly and dispersed dust, at the risk of contaminating the students. The faculty was shut down. For years, a squad of workers dressed like frogmen took over and peeled the buildings down to their core to make them salubrious.

That very same year, the Thetford Mines pits set production records, and chrysotile from KB3 was everywhere. In the air, the water, the ground, the backyards, the houses, the schools, the surface of the streets, even in Johanes Hansen's church.

The Thetford Mines Methodist Church and its parish house, built in 1956 by an entrepreneur named David Scott and situated in the Mitchell district, one of the most modest and most exposed to the exuberance of the mines, had an edifying list of construction specifications. "Exterior: major component, asbestos. Walls: asbestos. Roof: asbestos shingles." *Deo gratias*.

What in hell were God and Johanes Hansen doing in a place like that?

. . .

I arrived in Canada in 1976 on a flight loaded with jovial vacationers. I carried a khaki cloth travel bag, along with six miserable credits from the department of geography in Toulouse, not even enough to count as one year of university, and a little pocket money I won thanks to beginner's luck, one fanciful day, betting on the misery of the racehorses.

Sniffer dogs checked me out at the airport to make sure I was not transporting any powders, seeds or other food products that might be in violation of the strict protection laws set down by the Ministry of Agriculture. No bad seeds, nor good ones either, nothing likely to sprout, so I climbed onto the bus, seat D1, next to the window. At the very end of Route 112, after three hours and forty-five minutes of highway, as afternoon was expiring, I reached the depths of the devil's throat.

The pastor was waiting for me at the bus station. He looked younger, like a Dane enjoying a stay at a resort.

I took the man in my arms. I had probably never done that before. He drove me in his car, a 1966 Ford Bronco wagon that seemed to have been extracted from the strata of the Pleistocene, and whose mechanical design had obviously not been entrusted to Dr Felix Heinrich Wankel. The vehicle carried us to the parish house that belonged to the Methodist Church of Thetford Mines, where my father resided. The lot was dotted with pine trees that offered shadow to the facade and gave the building, which had a utilitarian look, an aspect more in keeping with the image a person might have of a place of spiritual offerings.

My father did not ask me about my trip, nor whether his ex-wife was still alive, or if her movie house was persevering in its explorations of the female throat. Not a word. His first words were, "Did you see those strip mines? I just can't get used to them." Later, after dinner, I thought of what he had said, and I asked him the only question that mattered, the one I should have asked the evening he informed us he was embarking on self-imposed exile to Canada. Instead of searching for a new job in such a far-flung territory, why had he not turned towards his native land, the Jutland peninsula? "I considered it, of course. But I realised I wasn't Danish enough for that anymore. Too much time in France, too much time with your mother. Too much time spent learning to write correctly, differentiating between all those words that seemed to be the same, and remembering all those grammatical rules. If I stopped practising, would I forget that when two verbs follow one another the second is always in the infinitive? Or that the past participle agrees when the direct object is placed before it? Here, I have discovered a little of both worlds, the language of your country and the climate of mine, and the fraternal nature of the women and men who live there. For our first evening, I really thought we could have talked about something else. For example, you could tell me in greater detail what got into you to go to the track and, on top of it, win the trifecta."

Officially, Johanes did not care for gambling, but I felt his excitement at the idea that his son, by entrusting his fate to Lady Luck, might win in a few seconds what he took three months to make. But when I offered to take him to see the ponies run, he closed up like a saloon door. "No servant can serve two masters": Luke 16:13. That was his unbending side returning, as he quoted Scripture with scientific precision, forever the wet blanket, the irritating pastor.

Last night, someone died in here. One inmate stabbed another in his cell. A guard told us about it. The murderer, whose name was Dusan, put a pillow over his cellmate's face and slit his throat, then waited until he stopped moving, until he had bled to death. When everything was quiet in the cell again, Dusan banged on the door to let the guards know what he had done. He did not try to resist. He described how he had made the knife: he had spent days filing down a fork handle on the concrete floor. The dead man's name was Sylvestre Aurèle. "I liked him alright, no problem, I liked him well enough, but I had to do it. He was Haitian and he'd completely changed lately. At night, he said stuff and did voodoo and threatened to cast a spell on me. He said that Xêvioso, the genie that fights thieves and criminals, would come and strike me down. I warned him more than once, I told him, 'Sylvestre, stop that or I'm going to have to kill you.' But he didn't believe me."

I hated when those things happened. They reminded me of what kind of place we were living in, and the nature of the men with whom I shared my meals and even, sometimes, a few moments of brotherhood, in the yard or the common room. The following days, when I crossed paths with them in the yard, I wondered what was going on in the backs of their minds, and what they had hidden in their pockets.

"I know Dusan, alright. He's not a bad guy, but everyone knows he's got a short fuse. When I used to pass out the pills, every night I gave him a double dose. If the doctors prescribed him that much, they must have known he was about to blow. But they're like the dentists, they don't care, they don't do anything. Tomorrow, instead of telling the police about the problem, how he was borderline, they'll keep their mouths shut. And Dusan will be charged with first degree. I don't believe Sylvestre wanted to cast a spell on him, and all that stuff. Sylvestre's one of the nicest guys in this prison, he's not aggressive at all, he's always apologising for everything. Sure, he was Haitian, so what? Haitians don't spend all day sticking pins in voodoo dolls. Tomorrow, I'm going to go tell the chief that with everything Dusan was taking, the guy couldn't think straight. That won't change anything, but I'm going to do it anyway."

As he gave me his class in Pen Psych 101, Patrick Horton paged through an old, worn-out porno mag that must have dated back to his teenage years. I have no idea how that kind of literature, forbidden by prison rules, could have slipped past the searches of our cell. Give credit to the benevolent complicity of the guards who, like offended virgins, closed their eyes to this relic of the past. After hesitating over who would be his chosen one, Patrick set his heart on a former splendour with whom he must have had a long-term relationship. He pulled down his zipper, declared a personal No Pants Day, and in his embarrassed killer's prudish little voice, asked, "Would you mind turning around a couple minutes? I'm going to jerk off."

Imprisonment lengthens the days, distorts the nights, stretches out the hours, it gives time a pasty, nauseating consistency. Every man feels like he is labouring through a thick layer of mud, and with every step he must pull his foot free to keep from bogging down in self-disgust. Prison buries us alive. Those with short sentences can maintain some hope. The rest lie in the common grave. If they ever get parole, they will breathe fresh air on the outside for a time, but will soon return to the house of the banished, where they are on first-name terms, and are treated like farm animals.

I miss my past life so intensely that sometimes I catch myself at night, clenching my teeth, grinding them together. My former life, the one I led when I was running the Excelsior, when Winona, in her Amelia Earhart costume, set down her single-engine Beaver on the Laurentian lakes, while Nouk, my dog for all eternity, swimmer of pools and sprinter of meadows, entertained long conversations with me, the subject of which only she knew. That life is gone, and when the prison doors open for me again, I will stand on the sidewalk in front of 800 Gouin Boulevard, and have to choose which way to go. My life sentence will continue in another form. And this time I will not have Patrick Horton's pre-teen magazines and postprandial bowel movements to take my mind off myself.

On Sunday, I dropped in on mass as performed by the prison chaplain. In a neon-lit room smelling of cresylic acid, a dozen inmates sat on cafeteria chairs, watching a poor overweight bugger whose every gesture spoke of his desire to throw off the tight sacerdotal robes that inhibited his movements. During the elevation, the ceremony intends for the officiant to raise the ciborium and hold it in his hands for the time it takes to recite the incantations. But in this case, the priest on duty, a prisoner of his obesity and the solid stitching on the sleeves of his disguise, could not lift the cup any higher than his chin. The move was completely without grace, and looked more like a demanding customer waving his empty glass in the barman's face.

The Catholic service, it has always seemed to me, issues from another era, another world, a dark age. Dressed up like Inca emperors, the officiants murmur overdone incantations in a dead language, mixing up water and wine, blessing a heel of bread, and when the stage known as "transubstantiation" is reached, they claim to have metamorphosed that old slice of dried flour into a dove from heaven. Even if no bird has ever left this room, every prisoner who ever watched the scene will swear to you that they saw it fly free. Because they do not feel like discussing it, because all you have to do is open your eyes at the right time, because they have a need to believe in this ancient story as, before them, their parents and the parents of their parents clung to it, and besides, long ago they were handed a practical piece of magic to quiet their doubts, and it is called faith.

Faith, the professional accessory that one day my father admitted he had lost, after torturing my mother's ears with it for years. Though, remember, he used to say he wanted to dwell within it, just for a moment, yes, just "a few hours spent in the perfection of faith".

"What the hell were you doing there? Since when do you go to mass? No shit, you jumped the track, you really ran off the rails. And in that crummy place that smells like piss. In a church, alright, just once, to see the show, the gold leaf, smell the herbs they burn, listen to the tunes, once, OK, I can understand. But in here, with that assembly of losers? And what about the priest? Shit, I can't stand him. I bet he tortures cats on the side. If they sent him here, you can be sure, no-one wants him anywhere else. Believe me, that crap ain't for us. Tell me, what did your Moses say to you?"

Moses turned to his meagre flock and solved his predicament with an all-purpose psalm. "Our soul is escaped as a bird out of the snare of the fowlers: the snare is broken, and we are escaped. Amen." That did not exactly promise results, but at least it was concise. It was a long way from my father's flowing preaching when, at the beginning of every chapter, the faithful felt the stirrings of spring, the ever-present murmur of nature, the rustling of the wind through the tall grass, the eager preparations of the robins perched on the low branches. The basis of his sermons, like the rest of his biblical bandying, would dissolve when exposed to reason, but his style was unique, with that simple and oh-so-Nordic manner he had of making you feel that life was everywhere around you, each thing had its sense and its value, a person had only to be attentive and look closely to understand that we all belonged to a gigantic symphony that, every morning, in its glittering cacophony, improvised its own survival.

I do not talk much about my mother. Maybe because I never understood why she left the big band so prematurely. On her bedside table, a long score of pills, a cantata of molecules expertly assembled to still the beating of hearts, and no more, not even a footnote left for her Swiss gentleman, her Danish ex-husband, or her almost-French son. Anna committed suicide at the age of sixty-one on May 14, 1991, the very day Jiang Qing, Mao Zedong's widow, put an end to her life at the end of a rope.

I wonder whether my mother was ill, if she was sad, too alone, if she had made the wrong choice with her Swiss gentleman, if she missed the movies, if she often thought about her parents' Citroën DS, if she was ashamed of me, if she had loved my father, if she had cheated on him a lot, if she had been afraid or felt regret after she swallowed those pills, if she remembered the squeaky parquet floor of our apartment, if she came and kissed me when I was a baby, if she held me close to reassure me, if she knew how beautiful I thought she was, and more brilliant than my father, and how much I liked all her films, if she remembered our trip to Denmark, if she still knew what *Jeg elsker dig mon søn* meant, if she could still translate it as "I love you, my son", if we really had something in common, she and I, that would keep us together for ever in some place, if she knew that in May '68 I had cut out and saved the dazibao that would have certainly made Jiang Qing smile at the end of her rope: "Godard, the biggest pro-Chinese Swiss asshole".

Time has passed, and when I think back, I believe that my mother would have made an excellent father. She would have been wonderful at pulling us behind in the wake she threw up, carrying us at top speed in the small craft she piloted heading straight for the reef, then dodging every depth charge like an expert, standing up to the naysayers. The very opposite of my father, who could never deal with more than one subject at a time. I always figured Anna had two brains. One was careful, thoughtful, given to analysis, research, concepts. And the other, always charged up, at full throttle, processing multiple levels of data, completing several tasks at once, shifting from one foot to the other, driving the whole convoy at breakneck speed. The very opposite of Patrick Horton's mother, mine would not have slipped a Bible into my pack before my departure for prison. Instead, as I went out the door, she would have said something encouraging and deeply caustic like, "People who work are bored when they're not working. People who don't work are never bored."

My father's little church in Thetford Mines was modestly built and resolutely Methodist. It was attached to the parish house where he lived, and was erected in 1957, designed by the architect Ludwig Hatschek. Using the appropriate terminology, it boasted a single nave, a rectangular course, an overhanging choir, a flat apse and a mitre-shaped vault. To put things in clearer language, with its evenly spaced ribs reaching to the ceiling, the church looked strangely like the inside of a ship that had capsized. With its peacefully luminescent stained glass, its pointed arched windows, its central aisle cushioned by purple carpet, its double row of pale wood pews, its cream-coloured powdered walls, its chandeliers like great jars filled with honey, Papa's Methodist church was made in his image: welcoming, placid, gentle and damned solid. It was located in the Mitchell district, where mostly English speakers lived, though his sermons delivered in his French accent caused no problems. Over a matter of a few months, Johanes accomplished a mighty feat: he adapted to his new community, and was adopted in turn. Every Sunday he filled his ship, and during the week, in the town, he took part in all sorts of activities that often went beyond his ministry. You would have sworn the man had been born a few pits away, a few craters from here. Once a week, on Sunday, he added an extra service that he called "the celebration of the miners". Like in a socialist realist film from the 1940s, men, grey with asbestos, still in their work clothes, emerged from the pits, entered the ship and floated off on a peaceful wave of words from the mouth of someone who promised them no more than a short respite and repose on the surface of the earth.

After a few months spent in his company, I understood that the pastor had found his place here. His was a world inhabited by people who, all in all, were not that different from the ones from his Danish peninsula, for they shared the same reciprocal benevolence. His universe could be described in the small catalogue of his daily life. A dependable 1966 Ford Bronco, the distant mountains, the abyss of the mines a few steps from the house, and all the opportunity in the world to write his notes, maintain his ship, celebrate what needed to be celebrated and, perhaps, from time to time think about a neighbourhood woman behind the conifers.

Such was the life of Johanes Hansen at the beginning of the year 1977.

Meanwhile, I rented an apartment on Notre-Dame Street and found work with a small general construction company. I became the right-hand man after only a few months. I learned most of the building trades in short order, and the wide variety of projects the company was involved in gave me the chance to pick up a number of new skills under the boss's watchful eye, give the best of myself. All of DuLaurier Construction fit into the company's Ford Econoline. At the wheel, Pierre DuLaurier, the father. Next to him, Zac and Joseph, his sons. In the back, with the machines and the tools, Joe Schmidt, chief apprentice, and me, one step below. During the summer, before the snow and freezing temperatures set in, we looked after the outside work, such as foundations and putting up exteriors. When winter came, we built a shelter for ourselves by fitting together glass panels, gyprock sheets and chimney sleeves, and by disciplining the disparate plumbing that had a tendency to run every which way. My hands bled, my knees swelled, my back ached, but I loved the work. No sooner had we finished a bathroom than we jumped over to a new house to build a clapboard garage, or redo the wiring damaged by a gang of squirrels. Zac and Joseph had deep respect for their father, a man who never raised his voice when he gave Joe instructions, and whistled continuously, melodies known only to him. I was given my tasks every morning, and told how to perform them without knocking out the district's power supply. I did not ask myself too many questions, as every day I took on my share of the missions.

The idea of living in a city submerged in asbestos, powdered by poison, haunted by asbestosis, did not bother me any more than it did the other Thetford Mines residents, who were born, grew up, learned, flirted, fucked, married, took out insurance, worked, divorced, socialised, found new bed partners, aged, coughed and died among the mountains and craters, the slag heaps and open pits.

Depending on the season, the pastor and I would go on excursions to Lake Memphremagog, which divides its waters between Canada and the United States, or the village of North Hatley with its Loyalist houses. We would always stop in Sherbrooke, home to Gérard LeBlond, the Methodist church organist. Every Sunday, he would drive up to Thetford Mines to illuminate the service with his music, which was more or less sacred. The man looked like a 1940s Hollywood heart-throb and, secretly, all the parishioners' wives of the age to commit the sins of the senses must have dreamed of him. But he was also an extraordinary organist, a musical phenomenon with arachnid fingers who spun infinite webs of notes on the double manuals of the Hammond B3 with its wooden pedal-board, set of drawbars, vibrato and chorus effects, ninety-one tonewheels and Leslie speaker. This incredible instrument, resolutely profane, came with the church, and usually made its voice heard with Procol Harum, the Doors, the Animals, Percy Sledge and James Brown. But when Gérard LeBlond sat down at the keyboard, well before the service, it seemed as though Jimmy Smith, Rhoda Scott and Errol Parker had come together to make God regret, had he existed, that he had not personally canonised Laurens Hammond, the inventor of this prodigious instrument. In the empty church, when LeBlond sat down at his worktable, when his fingers summoned forth all the devils of jazz, blues and swing, the old ship suddenly righted itself, the skies turned blue, happiness flooded into the naves and the tympanums, Jesus returned to his tomb, and Gérard, the prelate of Sherbrooke, reigned supreme in the glory of the skies.

Then, after a squall of riffs, everything slowly settled back to earth and took its assigned seat. In splendid unknowing, the first Methodists entered at the appointed time to the tempered sound of a Bach prelude. It was as if, every Sunday, the composer himself would sit down among the faithful to hear what was to come.

My father was quite aware that his organist's exceptional talent had an enormous impact on the popularity of his services. After a few years, it was hard to tell whether the word of God or the chords of the devil were drawing the crowds. And hearing the music was not good enough. The faithful arrived ever earlier to get the best seats. The spots in the first few rows gave them a breathtaking view of the fluid precision of the artist's fingers and the incredible ballet of his dancing feet, jumping and leaping from note to note on the two octaves of the pedalboard. Seen from behind, the movement of his legs looked like a lost man running, hesitating which way to go, one step to the right, changing his mind, veering left, choosing the middle path, then launching into that erratic choreography all over again. Though it seemed to lead nowhere, his footwork followed the path of the transcription rigorously, step by step. The virtuosity of LeBlond's toes was as legendary as that of his phalanges. In the community, he was known as "Four-Hands Gérard".

My father was more than a little proud of his charming partner, who, little by little, became his friend and his church's main attraction. In case he had any doubts, he just had to watch the crowd pressing around LeBlond after the service, at noon. Meanwhile, Johanes, slightly off to the side, shook hands with the few philistines who had never heard a note of music outside of a department store, a waiting room or a lift.

When we met up for a drink, Gérard could not help initiating us into the secrets of how the Hammond B3 was built. "It's absolutely incredible. A Rube Goldberg machine. Imagine ninety-one tonewheels, each with its own different set of gears. Then you make it revolve in a magnetic field. And there, a spool lined up with each magnet becomes the pickup for the variable magnetic field regenerated by the wheels, which themselves are made of ferromagnetic material. That was Laurens Hammond's secret, the alchemy he established between tonewheels, magnetic fields and pickups. Thanks to these electromagnetic alliances, and using the drawbars, you can play Patterson, Handel, Earland or Bach, each just as well as the other, by working the drawbars and avoiding the key clicks. Laurens was quite the odd bird. I read that he spent part of his childhood in France, and at fifteen, he offered to build an automatic transmission system for Renault. In America, in 1922, he invented a 3D vision system, created all sorts of weird clocks, bought a piano just to take it apart, and, with the help of his accountant, who presided over the keyboards in churches, he built an organ with pieces of wire, notched gears, magnets and spools hooked up to whatever he could imagine. That's how the brand was born. And while he was at it, in 1932 he produced the first polyphonic synthesiser, the Novachord. He was an incredible guy, inventing systems, one after the other. After taking on music, he patented new types of gyroscopes and then, before he died, he built a guided-missile system for the US army."

And what was the connection between the thunder of McNamara's bombs and the delicate breathiness of a B3 playing Bruckner's *Te Deum*? None, though the two dissonant and antinomian scores existed side by side in the brain of the same man like the erratic charge of a mind without a conscience banging away at the great pedalboard of knowledge.

With little sound and even less excitement, my life slowly came together in this odd little city. The finest days of spring gave downtown Thetford Mines a sprightly look and brought out the best of the handsome, British-style dwellings. I worked, I met women my age, I went canoeing on the lakes, and I even bought a car from Joseph, my boss's son, a little 1974 Honda Civic that weighed scarcely six hundred kilos, and whose motor, strangely enough, turned anticlockwise, a feature found in all the manufacturer's models.

At the end of a profitable and well-managed project, Pierre DuLaurier would take us all out to a restaurant. If it was winter, the menu featured something called *pâté chinois*, a local delicacy made of ground meat and corn, covered in melted cheese. The summer variation at the same place offered coleslaw, fried chicken in honey sauce and French fries. During these meetings around a Formica table, DuLaurier reinvented the world of construction, "kicked a couple of politicians in the balls", promised that next year we would expand and add more workers, then listened as his two sons gently mocked the little Honda they had palmed off on me. "It's cosy, and there's room, as long as you're not wearing a watch."

As the years passed, I became increasingly aware of the pastor's diminishing spiritual ardour, his weariness, the difficulty he had bringing the words of his books to life, his inability to pray and transmit what he was paid to. But he continued living within the boundaries, maintaining the parish house and the great ship he had been entrusted with. Every Sunday, Gérard did his duty and put on a show, and even if his Barnum & Bailey act meant little to him, Johanes continued to write, perhaps with even more care than before, telling the eternal tale of men, the world around them and its animals, often quoting the gospel according to Konrad Lorenz or Maurice Maeterlinck, going back to the beginning each time, to the very start, the day when heaven and earth had to divvy up the souls, with each summoned to choose between good and evil.

When he wanted to stave off the malaise of his position and his situation, my father would slip on his street clothes and visit the competition's sumptuous locale, the church of Saint-Alphonse at number 34 on Notre-Dame Street, two blocks from the post office and the bus station. He timed his arrival for a quiet hour and explored the place, hands crossed behind his back, adopting the pace a person might use when touring a museum. The building and its entire contents were listed among Quebec's cultural heritage sites, reputedly one of the richest and most beautiful in the province. Here, it goes without saying, there was not a trace of asbestos, nothing but the most noble materials. The chandeliers bearing one hundred candles, the jowly altars, the painted statues, the carved woodwork, the stone sculptures, the edifying canvases, the omnipresent decoration testifying to the opulence of the Catholic clergy who had long reigned as absolute masters over the bodies and souls of the people of this nation, and whose women, often mothers ten times over, fed the insatiable appetites of an ever more demanding Church. Everything the eye met, from floor to ceiling, everything that tinkled and shone, had not been raised to give praises to a God, but to bear witness to the work of the clergy, the pride and power of Rome.

And it was all very carefully done. A rounded vault, multiple caissons, a triple nave transept, solid wood and stone everywhere, pews as thick as tree trunks, all identical, the decoration baroque to the extreme. And artwork in every corner, in every form, paintings and embroidered fabric, altars with Swiss gold leaf, painted woodwork in a pale green shade, and the smell, that essence of well-maintained houses. Not to mention the eight decontamination stations, eight parlours of sin, eight intimidating confessionals whose dimensions and number suggested that Satan came to sup in the town every evening. The cherry on the sundae, perched in the top balcony, its pipes looking down on the sea of faithful, was a Casavant organ, opus 150, built in 1902, with twenty-one ranks, twenty-seven stops, plus another set of ranks using the pedals, and more pipes than anyone could need.

In this stucco universe, everything turned circles in my father's head, the capsized ship, the B3 with its pedalboard, the ferromagnetic tonewheels, Gérard's dancing feet, the pine pews, the bare walls, James Brown and Jimmy Smith ascending to the ceiling, the whole damn place going crazy while the Leslie speaker stirred the sauce, and outside, even the balsam fir trees shook their branches to the rhythm of the wind. The beat of this musical comedy restored a little of his faith in himself, and the desire, too, to try to recover the rabbit, the hat and, who knows, a little magic. Convinced that his rightful place was among the English-speaking folk of the Mitchell district, he returned, whistling, to his parish house, far from Rome, with her pomp and great works.

On the way back, walking with a pilgrim's step, he thought of those bankers' churches built like head offices, with neither humility nor reserve, whose stained glass was designed to display all that conspicuous consumption, the businessmen's trinkets once used to buy the land and memory of the native people.

January is endless and the polar vortex refuses to surrender its grip. At night, the temperature keeps dropping, but in the cells, the thermometer has stabilised at fifteen or sixteen degrees. The rivers have frozen and the waters of Niagara Falls have been caught in their flight. Patrick showed me photos from the paper. "They say it's a record, the ice has never been so thick. It's incredible. Like enormous stalactites. Notice that I didn't say stalagmites. A teacher taught us how to remember the difference between the two. A stalagmite goes up, it has to be mighty to hold up the ceiling. Smart, right? The picture makes me think of the fountain in the little park near where I used to live, except bigger. In the park, there was a statue of some chick practically naked holding a vase on her shoulder, and the water came out of it. When it froze, it didn't look like much – a little like the Niagara whatsits, but a whole lot smaller. When you see the size of the falls, and the weight, you wonder how it can keep standing. What do you think, when it starts to melt, is the ice going to fall all at once or little by little?"

This is typical of the circular pattern of Patrick's mind, which always concludes with an unexpected question. As surprising as a patch of black ice on the highway. Is there any possible answer?

Yesterday, in the visiting room, I had a rare moment of pleasure. The eighth visit from Kieran Read, the only person who over the last year has paid any attention to me, the one and only who, through this whole ordeal, has defended me. He was firmly opposed to my being fired, and supported my fragile position with my employer with the same conviction he displayed in the courtroom before the judge. His certainty did not do much good, and earned him strong enmity within the building.

Kieran Read was one of the sixty-three condo owners in Montreal's Ahuntsic district who had a piece of the Excelsior property. For twenty-six years, it was there that I practised the trade of superintendent, janitor, major-domo, nurse, confessor, gardener, psychologist, tech wizard, plumber, electrician, kitchen man, chemist, mechanic – in other words, the honourable guardian of this little temple. I held all the keys, or almost, and knew virtually all the secrets.

Mr Read lived in apartment 605, on the sixth and topmost floor. It looked out over the pool and garden, and during the evening hours it was bathed in soft light, with a splendid view of a large grove of maples and their wide crowns. Kieran Read, a Quebecker of British origin, spent most of his professional career in the United States and, until his retirement, practised a singular trade: evaluating the price of the dead. In his native tongue, he was what is called a casualties adjuster. He worked as a freelancer, hailed as needed, a taxi of misfortune, hired by insurance companies working to preserve their interests by bargaining down the worth of someone's dear departed after tragedy struck and the company had to indemnify the victim's family.

Kieran Read was one of the residents with the most seniority, and his lifestyle stressed discretion. And secrecy, his detractors would claim. He entertained no ongoing relationships with his neighbours and socialised very rarely in the common areas or around the pool. He was not frequently seen at condo meetings, and settled the bill for the charges as soon as he received it. The other residents watched him live his life in silence and retreat, and were all the more surprised when the man they hardly knew turned into a ferocious defender of the Excelsior's humblest servant.

When he returned from a mission, often late in the evening, Kieran would ring at my superintendent's apartment to chat a while and have a drink. I knew he did not feel like going up to the sixth floor right away to contemplate the file of the day, complete with a photograph of a decapitated corpse or a child crushed by a cement truck. He would knock at my door, sit down on the sofa, tell me of his trip, the purgatory of the boarding process followed by the turbulent flight, the cabin of some American airline outfit more suitable for sardines.

Then, after lingering over the Russian roulette of air travel, because sooner or later he had to cut to the chase, he would reveal the tragic content of his latest mandate, a new incursion into grief, pain and lethargy. With each visit, he told a horrible and unlikely story that he had to manage and assimilate as he rummaged through the pockets and the memories of the dead. Sometimes, the departed had lied, cheated, betrayed, concealed. Kieran's job was to make them speak. Though it had long been difficult for him to practise this trade, he told me how, over the years, he had learned to live in this world where the truth was often to be found halfway between the living and the dead, in the limbo of macabre accounting. Whenever my neighbour the adjuster returned from the road, the first words he spoke when he came through my door were always the same. "Today, Paul, I can be sure of one thing: I didn't make anybody happy."

Yesterday's visit comforted me and reconciled me with the world outside. The man trusted me, and that trust made me feel calm, peaceful and reassured. We talked about the Excelsior, the old version, from before, which very few knew. With its immature trees, miniature bushes, starter groves, timid grass with patches of alopecia, the garden was still only an experiment, demanding attention and care, and just enough water so that life could take root there. "We owe the garden to you, Paul. When I see the robust splendour it has taken on over the last thirty years, and when I remember how it was at the beginning, I can't believe it. Your father was a minister, wasn't he? He bequeathed the fingers of God to you. The guy who replaced you knows absolutely nothing about plants. He mows what grows and trims what sticks out. And that's all. He has no idea of the diseases that affect plants, their specific needs when it comes to water, and which species need to be bundled up for winter. Completely different from you. Completely. He has no regard for things, and he treats them with disrespect. The only time he seems to get interested in life, the only time some form of sensitivity enters him, is when he goes down to the garage to check the oil in his Chevrolet. I'm not making this up, Paul. The guy is obsessed, it's like a moment of religious ecstasy when he pulls out the dipstick and makes sure that the level is alright. Once I watched him as he was performing the operation, and it was obvious: the young man had attained his ultimate satisfaction. And that's not all. I noticed he has a particular attachment to the tyres of his car. He spends an enormous amount of time, not just cleaning them with a brush, but rubbing on some kind of shiny wax that gives them a totally ridiculous 'evening out' kind of look. The guy really loves his tyres, no doubt about it. Can you imagine me knocking at his door for a chat, the way we used to, but instead, discussing the relative merits of Goodyear all seasons versus the latest Firestone winter model? I will never forgive the president of the condo owners' association for firing you. And for replacing you with an idiot obsessed with lubricants and inner tubes."

Hearing Kieran's voice again, his terribly British bantering tone, his botanical compliments twinned with the mischief he played on my successor, all that did me a considerable amount of good and made my prison routine almost tolerable, turning the cold into a passing anecdote, transforming Patrick's bowel movements into something more or less entertaining. Just now, Patrick took up position, and after exerting extraordinary effort, was richly rewarded. All through the operation, he stared at me, wearing that awkward, perplexed look that dogs often display when they are caught in the midst of their business.

And the Organ Fell Silent

THE YEARS PASSED. The pastor respected the terms of his mandate to the letter, and clung to his English parishioners, who, for their part, attended church mostly to see LeBlond's malleoli twist on the pedalboard. Meanwhile, I ascended a rung in the brotherhood of builders, since Pierre DuLaurier was now entrusting me with small worksites, as well as the basic training of a new apprentice, Bob Woodward, who stubbornly refused to speak anything but English. All day long, "fuck" and "shit" flew through the air, which is never a good sign. But Bobby, as the boss called him, despite his enormous shortcomings and high opinion of himself, seemed to enjoy a degree of impunity.

At age twenty-six, I had to face the facts: the Thetford girls were not knocking at my door. I made up for that lack with intensive canoeing sessions as soon as the weather permitted. I would launch my boat in the morning and return in the evening, paddling all day long on the lacquered skin of the lakes: Magog, Massawippi, Aylmer and Saint-François. They were all different, with their own smells and wind patterns, and the invisible fingers of their currents. But all were bearers of a vital force and a primal happiness that gave me an unbending desire to reach the far end, to succeed, whatever it took, however long it was.

As I rowed, my father preached, Gerard pedalled and the asbestos frayed, something was happening in the province, a groundswell that shook the federal state and made the British throne tremble. Quebec began a referendum process to gain independence, wave *au revoir* to Ottawa and take French leave of London, to live among its own kind for the rest of its life. Carefully packaged and wrapped by politician René Lévesque and his Parti Québécois, the referendum question on the province's independence was placed at the foot of the federal Christmas tree on December 20, 1979, and also in the hands of the government of Pierre Elliott Trudeau, who, though a Quebecker himself, was fiercely opposed to a divorce disguised as "sovereignty-association". In any case, everyone soon discovered that they would be choosing a future based on a text written by a gang of Jesuits from the Parti Québécois, one of whom was later suspected of being a mole for the federal government. "The Government of Quebec has made public its proposal to negotiate a new agreement with the rest of Canada, based on the equality of nations; this agreement would enable Quebec to acquire the exclusive power to make its laws, levy its taxes and establish relations abroad – in other words, sovereignty – and at the same time to maintain with Canada an economic association including a common currency; any change in political status resulting from these

95

negotiations will only be implemented with popular approval through another referendum; on these terms, do you give the Government of Quebec the mandate to negotiate the proposed agreement between Quebec and Canada?"

Even the house of DuLaurier would have refused to build anything based on such a clumsy foundation, especially considering that the architect of this scrapheap, at the height of his amateurish incompetence, used the semicolon three times, the punctuation of embarrassment and doubt, revealing a timid mind hesitating between the temptation to finish it off once and for all, or continue the sentence to see where it would take us.

On Tuesday, May 20, 1980, after a rough campaign that split families down the middle, the people of Quebec cast 2,187,991 ballots saying, *Non, merci!* By 59.56 per cent to 40.44 per cent, they rejected the idea of entrusting their future to three semicolons.

As permanent residents and not citizens, my father and I did not participate in the vote. On the other hand, in the DuLaurier family, who had hammered home the hope for independence, everyone was devastated. They all sat in front of the television, except for Woodward, who was probably out celebrating the federalist victory with a few hacks who still belonged to the Crown. At one point that evening, René Lévesque appeared on the screen. Had he thought out his words in advance, or were they inspired by his supporters' mix of pride, sadness and anger? The people watching television that night did not ask themselves the question. When they heard this man say to them, "If I understand you correctly, you are telling us next time!" they looked to one another and saw their eyes were filled with tears.

My father used the five days before his next service to write a sermon with no semicolons, largely inspired by Lévesque's message of hope. The pastor's lengthy discourse praised the primordial role that faith plays when a person embarks on the battle of a lifetime, the never-ending, always difficult quest to conquer grace or, here, in the subtext, independence.

My father and faith. He had never talked about it so much until he lost it. "Even when you are down to the ground, and think it is all over, and have nothing but doubt, rise up and believe, believe above all and against the odds, for the Lord is with you, it is His voice telling you there will be a next time, and if needed, a time after that, and at the end of the end, at the end of the long path, you will finally enter the House." Nothing very new, classic and conventional, but five days after Lévesque's brief epistle, this ode to my father's stubborn hope sent shivers down the English spine, and the faithful did not linger in front of the church that Sunday.

In 1980, the mines were still active and men were gaily pumping away at the Pleistocene. To go deeper, and quarry out the pits and uncover new veins, the companies used dynamite. Huge explosions regularly shook the earth and the city that had been placed on top of it. As time went by and the explosives nibbled away at the surface, gaping holes reached closer to the houses and inhabited areas. It happened quite often: scattered by the indiscriminate use of dynamite, a rain of earth, rocks and pebbles fell on the nearby houses, the people who lived in them, and their cars.

At the end of the 1960s, an event occurred that, with its violence, foreshadowed the new methods and priorities of the world to come. The mining interests claimed they wanted to protect the residents from danger, but the reality was different. The companies had discovered a new vein under the houses in the Saint-Maurice district, and the mineral was too good to leave in the ground. The *tabula rasa* approach was adopted. One by one, the companies moved the houses, garages, water mains, streets, people, furniture, goods and memories, and deposited everything in a vacant wasteland at some distance further on, all the elements of the former neighbourhood thrown together every which way, leaving the demolition crews with only the carcass of a church too complex to dismantle, as well as a string of old administrative buildings which were razed to the ground. The sector was deemed ready for explosives. Or almost, because as the delays added up, and one study contradicted the next, the site was never exploited.

Though it stood at the confluence of the King, Bell, Beaver and Johnson pits, the Mitchell district remained where it was, and had to get used to the dust and the bombardment. This belligerent cohabitation continued until one day half a roof collapsed under the impact of a robust fibrous meteorite rising up from the centre of the earth. Suddenly everyone became aware of the danger of living in the line of fire of blind snipers equipped with large calibre weapons.

Hurried meetings were held, and promises made to keep the operations that scraped out the earth as far from the houses as possible. The companies offered a further symbolic safety measure: they would sound a high-powered siren fifteen minutes before blasting. This procedure was soon dis-continued, but I was lucky enough to witness the panic caused by these shrill trumpets of death.

The people in the affected neighbourhoods, who had previously lived in indifference and disregard for risk, inexplicably panicked once the alarm was installed and triggered. Each time, people would hurry home and close their doors and windows, protecting everything that could be saved, far more terrified by the pre-emptive howls of today's beast than by the actual explosions of the past. My father was among those who put his affairs in order every time the harbinger of the end of the world sounded.

Sometimes, for meteorological reasons or operational convenience, the pits were dynamited on Sunday mornings. Several times, my father went and complained to the companies about the disruption of his services. They promised to look into it. The following weekends, the explosions increased in intensity, and with them the terrifying groans from the depths of the earth. One Sunday when I was visiting him, I arrived in the ship in the middle of his sermon, while Gerard LeBlond worked the drawbars for the "full organ" effect. To mention that the pastor was speaking of doubt and faith would be superfluous, since those two themes represented nine-tenths of his interventions. That day, he was going about his business, and had reached the heart of his argument, urging on the listeners, then cajoling them, modulating the special effects, whispering praise, condemning sin, swimming in his own words as if floating on water. I remember at one point in a story about the spirit of tolerance and acceptance of others, he paused, a lengthy silence during which he appeared to gaze at each and every one of his followers. Back in Toulouse, I had seen him use the same trick to capture his flock's attention. When he considered that all the conditions were met, he delivered a message he probably never imagined would have such impact: "It is in the silence of the stones and the forests that we sometimes hear the murmur of the gods." No sooner had he uttered the last word of that sentence than the siren began to roar like blasphemy. He went no further, and no-one knew what the deities were really saying – the use of the plural must have surprised many – as they whispered in the ears of the tenants of this life. He hastily folded his notes and entreated everyone to rise and go in peace, but hastily, if you please, before the world came crashing down on their heads. With a sense of humour and impeccable timing, the organ master provided a soundtrack for the growing panic that overtook the exodus. With all four hands, he performed "Nearer, My God, to Thee", a Christian hymn inspired by the poet Sarah Flower Adams, and famous for allegedly having been played to the very last note during the sinking of the RMS *Titanic*. That Sunday, fifteen minutes after the alert, the explosion occurred. Apart from a few spare stones and gravel that did not even scratch the solid hull of the ship, nothing more than a fine snow of asbestos flakes slowly descended upon us.

Watching a hockey game in prison is a sport in its own right, and it requires some preparation if you intend to play alongside Patrick Horton. When the Montreal Canadiens score, he throws himself on his comrades and shakes them until their teeth rattle. When the Canadiens get beaten, he whales away at those friends as if they were punching bags. Tonight, we watched the Canadiens against the Toronto Maple Leafs, two rivals whose games rarely end without some subtle high-sticking and resounding body checks. Though they helped their team win, two Leafs players, Phaneuf and Armstrong, seemed particularly virulent. "Virulent? Virulent? You've got to be kidding! I don't know why I talk hockey with you, you don't know anything about it. Don't fuck with me. Phaneuf is the biggest son of a bitch who ever took to the ice. He's a slasher. Don't waste your time with a stick, use a base-ball bat or a meat cleaver on him. Tonight, he was the one who stirred up all the shit. Same with Armstrong. He's the number two slasher. If Phaneuf misses you, Armstrong will impale you. Those guys should go play on the ice floes with polar bears, not on a rink, not in the NHL."

To unwind after the game, we watched a documentary on Celtic sports and caber-tossing. Guys throw logs five or seven metres long and a hundred or a hundred and ten kilos in weight as far as they can. "Instead of hassling the trees, they should toss Phaneuf and Armstrong."

I remember watching a lot of hockey games in 1969 with my father during the World Cup in Sweden. In Toulouse, of course, the sport was not very popular, but Johanes with his Scandinavian origins did not miss a single game, which is how I familiarised myself with the rules of the sport. There was a historical encounter between the USSR and Czechoslovakia less than a year after Russian tanks invaded Prague. An amazing match, a real war on ice, and the Czechs won four to three, but because of a better overall goal average, the Russians were crowned world champions. Contrary to tradition, the players refused to shake hands at the end of the game. As the medals were being handed out, and "The Internationale" played, Czech television cut the sound. And when the Soviets took to the podium, the visuals disappeared, too.

I tried to tell my cellmate about this historical game. "Why are you telling me this crap? I don't give a shit about your '69 Russkies. I know all about that. What does it have to do with Phaneuf and Armstrong? Where's your father from? Denmark? Fucking perfect timing. You know who the Danes played their first official game against in 1949? Canada. And do you have any idea what the score was? Forty-nine to nothing. So don't get all educated with your Russian tanks and shit. In history and politics, OK, I know, I'm a marblehead. But when it comes to hockey and the Canadian team, I know every score, every record, every player. Go ahead, ask me a question. How many times world champion? Twenty-four. The Olympics? Gold seven times. Biggest victory? I told you, against your old man's jokers. Biggest defeat? In 1977, against the fucking Soviets, 11–1. All-time leading scorer? Wayne Gretzky. Is that good enough for you? Get the picture? Now go clean up your room." Then he made that ridiculous face you see in sports, his right hand pulling down on an invisible alarm handle, while he wrinkled up his forehead and bit his lower lip. "If you really want to understand hockey, buddy-boy, you have to be born into it. You have to be five years old and freeze your feet on the neighbourhood rink till you can't feel your toes, then go home and get a slap in the face because you left your stick in the driveway. When you play, you've got to know how to take it and how to dish it out, and you have to skate like hell and make your mark with every shift. Have you ever even been on skates?" I was afraid to tell him the truth, and since he asked me to, I went and cleaned up my room.

Who could have imagined, in Thetford Mines, that things would evolve the way they did, and that Pastor Hansen would go adrift so suddenly and so unpredictably? In January 1982, he received an urgent summons from his employers, the Quebec and Sherbrooke Presbytery of the United Church of Canada. To support him during the ordeal he was about to go through, and for which I felt partly responsible, I drove him to the meeting and parked the car not far from the building where a kind of ecclesiastical tribunal would learn of his deeds and decide upon his fate. During the hour the hearing lasted, I sat behind the wheel, listening to the radio and wondering how all this could have happened, how Johanes had, in one year, accumulated that much debt and ruined the future of his mission to such an extent.

As he returned to the car, I saw he was walking as close to the building as possible, along the pavement, as if wanting to seek shelter from something. The car door slammed shut. He ran his hands over his face and rubbed his eyes. "I'm glad you came with me, I'm glad you came." As he sometimes did during his sermons, he held the silence. This time, it was not a pulpit trick or a flourish of oratory. His lungs were out of air, his heart out of strength, his mind unable to follow a coherent train of thought. He turned his face towards me. "They gave me six months to pay back what I owe, put the church's accounts in order, and give back the keys. If not, they'll press charges." He lifted his palms heavenwards. "There was nothing else they could do."

It had all started a year earlier, I believe, in the early winter of 1981. After the first snow, the cold began to crack the roads and the days shortened abruptly, as if they were in a hurry to dissolve into darkness. With the change of season, something in us changed as well, a vague weariness set in, and with it a sense of melancholy. I was very sensitive to that. To shake off the depressing atmosphere, I suggested to my father that we go to Quebec City and spend an evening at the Palais Central, the track that featured harness racing. Seen from the outside, with its two bell towers, central arcade and symmetrical architecture, the large main grandstands bore a strange resemblance to the facade of a bullfighting ring in northern Spain. Inside, everything was more conventional, with a 70-foot-long track built on a sandy foundation, covered with clay and ashes, and open nearly year-round, since, to keep the bettors happy, the owners had heating installed in the stands. That evening, there were seven races on the card.

It did not take much energy to convince my father to come with me. The man who, not long before, forbade himself from serving two masters, took quiet leave from one to go for a jaunt and rub shoulders with the other. Before each race, depending on the colour of the jockey's cap or silks, the elegance of a sulky, the coat of the animal about which he knew nothing, Johanes would choose a horse and run down to the betting window as if his life depended on it, pull out his money, and wager on an unknown mane or a random stride, with a drive and a faith that did not suggest for an instant that he was going through a crisis of trust in himself and his Saviour. Then, four steps at a time, he ran back to his spot in the stands. That night, the heavens closed their eyes on his infidelity; my father's record was astonishing. Four winning horses, two places, and one disqualification due to irregular conduct.

In my little Honda, I drove a wealthy man back home, a man transfigured by the happiness of having played a good trick on Lady Luck, who, for once, decided to smile upon him. Four or five hundred dollars' worth of winnings, the thrill of the race, the smell of beer and cigars, the shouts in the stands, the cold outside, the fire within, the uncertainty until the last moment, the imbalance of chance – that was all it took for the pastor to realise that the racetrack at the Palais Central opened up a field of possibilities that nothing in the Bible had ever suggested.

The next week, same day, same time, same place, same races. Johanes insisted we make the trip. During the ride, he told me he had truly enjoyed his first experience, which he found very "exciting". An unusual word in my father's mouth. I noticed the large leather case hanging from a strap around his neck. "Binoculars. To keep better track of the race.

I noticed that almost everyone has a pair." A further surprise: on the forecourt of the racetrack, my father took a chequered cap out of his pocket and carefully fitted it on his head, as if this accessory crowned the beginning of a new life.

In his new livery, which did not look so bad on him, Johanes renewed his lease with the trotting gods who once again served him beyond all expectations. During the last race, his eyes glued to his binoculars, his voice rose in intensity as his favourite moved towards the front. And when he took the lead, the pastor sinned for the first time. "Go on, damn it, go!" In the car on the way home, he told me that, when you thought about it, gambling was a wonderful profession. Sitting and watching, betting, winning, going home. He did not seem to imagine that any risk was involved – that of losing, for starters. He did not consider he would ever be betrayed by his lucky star. That night, I understood that the devil had gotten his foot in the door. I never foresaw that Johanes himself would open it so wide for Old Scratch.

My father wrapped up the winter season at the Palais Central, the only racetrack in Quebec that could operate during the cold months. As far as I know, he did not miss a single session and continued to make a profit through the whole year, though a few solid setbacks did shake the optimism of his accounts. I am using the wrong word, for during this period my father never kept a ledger. In that way, he belonged to that terrible category of gamblers who remember only their victories, and forget their losses as soon as they have been suffered. As long as there was money in his pockets, this system would work, more or less.

In the spring, my father discarded Quebec City and turned to Trois-Rivières and its large professional racetrack built in 1830, where, in the early days, men competed against horses. Later, trotters, sulkies and flat races took over, bringing together the best thoroughbreds from Canada and the United States. The societies behind these races included the Three Rivers Turf Club, to flatter the English, and the Saint-Maurice Turf Club, to console the French. Since its creation, and up until recently, this racetrack knew its share of dark days, including three violent fires that destroyed the stables. The last two resulted in the death of one hundred and seventy-four horses that were locked in their stalls. My father had read up on his new place of perdition, and seemed proud that King William IV of England had journeyed there in 1836 to offer a fifty-guinea purse to the winner of a flat race. Perhaps it was the prospect of such rewards that gave the pastor new faith in these saddled animals filled to the gills with trama-dol, codeine, ketoprofen, clenbuterol and stanozolol. Johanes swept away these prescriptions with a broad gesture, main-taining that such practices were unlikely today, given the rigorous testing and chemical analyses. Within a few months, my father had become a caricature of the *turfiste*, with his binoculars around his neck like a bib, his six-flapped cap, his first-hand information probably gleaned from around the par-ish house, and his blind faith in a dubious institution long since blacklisted by every United Church Conference in the world.

As in Quebec City, he started out by breaking the bank, winning or placing through early spring. In record time, he assimilated the last names of the jockeys, the reputations of the owners, the names of the horses and the first names of the cashier women. By dint of seeing him come and go among the paddocks, the presentation ring and the odds board, some of them began calling him "Mr Johanes" as they handed him his slips. But by the beginning of summer, Mr Johanes' lucky star began a long eclipse. Trotters, flat racers and sulkies turned to some newcomer, an ordinary guy who knew nothing about the science, who had not yet purchased a cap or a pair of binoculars, sitting in the stands somewhere with his youngest son, who had invited him to enjoy the fine weather by spending an afternoon at the races.

The pastor's pockets began to empty. Like a pump that is primed mechanically, the flow of his losses accelerated. A few successes, a place here, a win there that did not produce much, certainly not enough to staunch the bleeding.

At church, preoccupied by his problems on the oval track, the pastor was sloppy with his sermons, neglected the service, arrived late for celebrations, forgot appointments and was less and less concerned with Gérard's music, though the man could see that something was wrong. He opened up to me. I had to tell him the truth. Overnight, my father had become a horse lunatic, a compulsive gambler for whom money, devoid of all value, was simply a vector, a way of reaching that adrenaline rush accessible only during "those few seconds in the perfection of the home stretch".

The old faith had gone out the window. A new one replaced it. My father still had the need to believe.

When I explained this to Gerard, I remember how he

looked at me and the strange thing he said. "I would rather it were that. I was afraid it was a woman."

The woman was not yet there. Though no-one could have guessed it at the time, she was already moving through the corridors of destiny.

My father was much loved by his lady parishioners. He treated them with empathy and great respect, encouraged them in their abilities and studies, and never forced them into a moral corset. He was the exact opposite of the country's Catholic clergy. Until the beginning of the 1960s, their doctrine was simple: procreate like rabbits, go forth and multiply and head off the English, contain them, strengthen the armies of Rome, weaken the legions of the anti-Papist Protestant devils. Like travelling salesmen, back then priests dropped in on families to bless their houses and visit the mothers, inciting them to rev up the life cycles, set aside the exhaustion of their bodies, and engage in sacred fornication, with neither truce nor respite, night and day if necessary, as long as something issued from it in the end. Litters of twelve children were common. Women emerged from the confessional in tears after being lectured and labelled bad Christians for having given birth to merely seven children in thirteen years of marriage. Returning home, as atonement they commanded their husband to get to work, pell-mell. For the Lord was waiting, and the Church was an impatient mistress. It was also good form to reserve a boy from the lineage to take up the cause, stay on the straight and narrow, and enter orders. The clergy's tribute, God's share.

Women's collective memory kept those days alive: their

children hastily conceived beneath the crucifix, their bodies grown weary before their time. A pastor like Johanes Hansen, who was benevolent and tolerant, though living for some time now with a cavalcade of tiny horses turning circles in his head, was deeply appreciated.

At the end of the summer, the fall was vertiginous and the losses in Trois-Rivières swelled from week to week. The pastor had entered the vortex of the vanquished, the black hole that inexorably swallows up those who have lost too much to give up. Despite everything, he was convinced in his heart that luck and the horses would eventually turn his way. The very elixir, the cocktail of catastrophe.

At the beginning of September, my father opened up to me about his difficulties and explained he was going to take out a loan from the Caisses Desjardins credit union to reimburse what he had "borrowed" from the operating budget of the church and the parish house. What he neglected to tell me was that the loan agreed by the Caisses was much higher than his debt. He intended to use the substantial difference between the two sums to remake his life, repay the church and the bank, absolve his own sins, and restart his career as a Danish pastor without the benefit of binoculars, a cap, racing forms or tramadol.

In a way, I could say my father fulfilled half his commitments. Once he received his cheque, he never set foot at a racetrack again, and returned to the church all he had embezzled, down to the last penny. In one day, Johanes Hansen repaid his debt, his *culpa*, and now was simply one debtor among so many others in one of the four hundred and twenty-two branches of the solid financial institution founded in 1900 by Alphonse Desjardins, which produced an average profit of more than a billion dollars a year.

The intoxicating figures may have given Johanes the feeling that it was time to return to the world of winners, sell off his liabilities, and beat down his interest payments. It was an easy matter to slip his hand into his pocket, padded as it was with the surplus from his loan.

One evening, he put on his charcoal-grey suit, closed the parish house door, climbed into his Bronco, and, under a rain of autumn leaves, drove until he could see in the darkness the shimmering lights of the Montreal skyscrapers, exhaling the white smoke of their breath as if it were midwinter. Johanes Hansen, as he had sworn to his Creator, did not go to the races. He crossed the Champlain Bridge, took the Bonaventure Expressway, and turned right towards Île Notre-Dame, where a low industrial building awaited him. Its scattered shards of light reflected off the river, and the building seemed to be there for him personally, the little pastor from Thetford Mines with his church of asbestos. The former warehouse, which had been converted into a gambling den, lay a few hundred metres from what would become, some ten years later, the enormous Montreal Casino that had been fitted into the empty shell of the former Quebec and French pavilions designed for the 1967 World's Fair.

The Moneymaker gambling club was a long way from shiny opulence. A gambler from Trois-Rivières had recommended the lair to my father. He claimed he had won enough in one evening of throwing dice to buy a Mercury Marquis.

There were fifteen tables or so, where a man could alternate between roulette, blackjack and craps. A hall was lined with slot machines, and a dedicated room accommodated poker players. One hundred and fifty or two hundred people in all, disparate furniture, cut-rate croupiers, second-hand equipment, overly bright lights, acrid smoke. Everything was ready, the decor laid out beautifully, the extras stood where they should be. All that was missing was the pastor of Thetford Mines, the Dane of little faith, who, for the occasion, had put on his dark suit, the one he usually wore to bury the dead.

The Stations of the Cross were played out in two stages, two inexorable, predictable steps, described in every survival manual. He began with luck smiling sweetly upon him, though it was no more than mercantile flattery, an insignificant win at the roulette wheel, a handshake to restore confidence. Then a second modest victory, conceded almost inadvertently, but which made him feel better, even in his funeral suit. On this evening of redemption, strangely confident, my father had brought the entirety of the excess funds he had borrowed. A large sum. In less than two dreadful hours, the precision mechanics of failure meticulously nibbled away every last penny of his illusory savings. The dice slaughtered my father. Throw after throw, the cubes showed the wrong face, fun turned to massacre, his dollars disappeared down a thirsty spillway. In the end, instead of leaving with a Mercury Marquis, he had to admit defeat and leave the stage at the wheel of his old Bronco, his mind unhinged, stripped bare, laminated, his eyes unfocused, barely able to follow the dotted line on the road home.

Reason would have dictated that this trip have no follow-up. That my father stay in his house at the foot of his church and brood over his pastoral errors. Then promise himself that in the future he would play up to his English parishioners, polish his B3, dust off his asbestos, pay back Desjardins and, most of all, never again frequent gambling circles and racetracks.

The day after his debacle, after a long night filled with fleeting and contradictory thoughts, he parked his Ford under the highly deceptive, bluish Moneymaker sign. During his insomnia, when melatonin deserted him, he imagined everything and its opposite. The wee hours suggested the last chance solution, undoubtedly risky, but he claimed to have analysed its probabilities, and that it offered the best capital-to-risk ratio. Of course, all this was based on nothing more than one of those endless exercises in self-persuasion without which casinos would have long since disappeared. Superstitious like all gamblers, he left his funeral suit in the closet and chose a less conservative outfit which had often supplied good results at the racetrack.

To fuel the fires that evening, he plundered the collection boxes in his church. By that, I mean, for the second time, he diverted the entire operating budget of his parish, stole and scraped together everything that could be scraped.

Seeking shelter in his strategic fantasies, my father followed a protocol that would have terrified any gambler with a shred of sense. He split his money into four equal parts and bet on four different games, choosing red or black every time, and paying no mind to any other combination.

Johanes would either double his money or lose everything.

He chose to entrust his future to double or nothing, even though, in his situation, hoping to double anything belonged to the realm of dreams.

At 11.10 p.m., he put the first quarter of his fortune on red, and was at once thwarted by black. He went for a short walk around the room. Ten minutes later, he confirmed his first choice of colours. The marble spun on the wheel and, like a bird of prey, swooped down onto the twenty-nine, perhaps the blackest of blacks. "Oddly enough, I wasn't afraid, and I didn't doubt either. I was completely convinced that all this shit was going to stop, it couldn't be any other way, bad luck would end up attacking someone else and leave me alone. I would pull through in the end, the way it happened in Trois-Rivières, on the home stretch of the last race."

With every move he made, the dealer seemed truly astonished by the amount my father was betting, and his stubborn refusal to break it down into multiple combinations, instead of concentrating everything on a single binary hope.

At 11.30 p.m., red was chosen and black showed itself.

My father was entering his own personal home stretch. He was sure he had the resources to move up through the field and catch everyone at the finish line, the way a certain Walter Season had in the last race of the summer. Shot up with every legal and illegal substance, the horse had made up the distance, neck after neck, chest after chest, as trails of white foam flew from its mouth in the heat of its effort. It pulled its cart the way it had always done, paying no mind to the guy in the polka-dot silks who, behind him, was going crazy on the sulky, which seemed to go airborne with every stride. The jockey shouted and used the whip, though his efforts were needless, since the horse knew perfectly well what it had to do: catch them all, one after the other, and thrust its head straight and high, raised and victorious, for the photo finish.

Everything my father had learned from Walter Season could not save him that night. By 11.45, it was over. Nothing he believed in had happened. No reversal of fortune, no miraculous return. On the photo finish, all that could be seen was a pastor timidly choosing red and the hand of God clearly sliding the ball onto black.

The second the wheel stopped spinning, my father became a petty Danish thief, an inconvenient permanent resident who would soon be summoned and cast out by his diocese, then sued by his bank, and in the end face legal proceedings.

"I remember a strange thing happened. When I left the table, a very pretty woman came up to me and took me by the arm. We walked across the room. I was in a state of shock, floating in a world I did not recognise. The woman asked me my name and what I did for a living. I said I was Johanes Hansen, a pastor in Thetford Mines. She took my face in her hands, looked at me as if I were an orphan, and kissed me on the mouth, a long kiss. I stood there, arms at my sides, my eyes wide open. Then she pulled away and said, 'If he sees you, may God bless you.' After that, I swear I don't remember a thing, not how I left the Moneymaker, nor how I drove home."

During the days that followed, the appearance of that mysterious woman held my father's attention much more than the procession of legal challenges that his losses on Île Notre-Dame had caused. She would continue to haunt him through the endless night that awaited.

His peers had given him six months to pay off his debt, but the reprieve was much too short, since the Caisses Desjardins would not lend him another dollar. He absolutely refused to consider asking his family in Skagen for help. He decided that all he could do was crouch below decks and wait to go down with his ship.

For several weeks, I searched heaven and earth for an acceptable way out of the situation. I counted up my savings and considered taking out a loan to get Johanes afloat again. But the hull was taking on water, and my meagre pile of pennies could not plug the breach.

I promised my father never to reveal the extent and amount of his losses. All I can say is that they were far beyond the scope of a pastor's lifestyle.

Two months after the debacle, my father returned to the Moneymaker a couple of times. Gambling was not his intent. He was hoping to find the woman who had put him in God's hands, then disappeared. But in that warehouse, he met only men like himself, who had come in search of something they would never find.

On Sundays, Johanes went on celebrating the service as if nothing had happened. Gérard was posted at the Hammond organ, and the English faithful occupied their pale wooden pews. Knowing he was damned, my father wrote sermons the likes of which no-one had ever heard. His texts went beyond the limits of the Church, they embraced the vagaries of destiny, and placed us in our rightful spot in the buzzing brothel of life, on equal footing with the larch and the tapir, tenants of the same cell, worried about the future, all of us trying to believe in the benevolence of the gods even if our instincts whispered the opposite.

For the first time since I was a child, I returned every Sunday to listen to him. And, I must admit, I also came to observe the embarrassed and growing scepticism of this conservative English-speaking outpost as it listened to his liberation theology.

Since his interview in Montreal and with his imminent dismissal looming, the pastor felt free of all his contracts with both the Church and God, since the latter had let him down at the worst possible moment: the home stretch. He let himself go, surrendering with neither restraint nor fear, chattering on about trees, men and beasts, relating the story of the fishermen of Jutland, and the opposing currents that tried to pull them apart, and fish everywhere, whose dead bodies would one day drown the bell tower of the church buried in sand. The congregation sensed he was throwing himself off the top of a tall building and, as he stood before us, he was delivering the visions born of his fall. The most astonishing thing was that, most of the time, his epic tales lured his followers into his world. Everyone seemed captivated, with the exception, quite possibly, of those stiff-necked Brits.

His sermon of March 14, 1982 was as magical and vaporous as those he had pronounced before. No doubt tipped off by the faction of the club who had denounced the heretic of Thetford Mines, soon to be expelled, a representative of the

Presbytery of the United Church of Canada came to see for himself how far the pastor had drifted. He left upset by what he heard, and then witnessed.

On that Sunday, the sermon was concerned with the burdens and woes that families pass on from one generation to the next, stories about which we know little but must still acknowledge, carry then fill with our own sorrows before passing them on to the next in line. All this rattled about in the confusion and chaos of my father's fever, and the congregation felt he was trying to set the record straight, once and for all.

"And now, I would like to tell you something. This is no doubt one of the last times I will stand before you. I came to Thetford Mines because I was no longer wanted elsewhere. And I will leave this place for the same reason. I have sinned, twice. Twice, I have been driven out. You will certainly learn some unpleasant things about me. All of them will be true. Once again, I will have nothing to say in my defence. But I want you to know that in all the years I have been with you, I have acted as a dedicated and loyal employee. Even if that description might seem strange now. Even if faith has long since deserted me. Even if praying has become impossible. Soon you will have the time and leisure to judge and condemn me. I ask you to keep in mind these few words I learned from my father, and that he would use to minimise a person's sins: 'Not everyone lives in the world the same way.' If he sees you, may God bless you."

The pastor's knees bent ever so slightly, and his hands clutched the pulpit. Always the faithful partner, Gérard began a prelude that they had chosen together, and the Leslie speaker spread armfuls of sound over all men of goodwill.

Johanes looked into the assembly as if searching for a friend in a crowd of strangers. He opened his mouth, perhaps he had neglected to tell us something, other words still needed to spill out. Then his hands slipped along the wall of the world, his legs gave out, and he collapsed.

The church drew a breath of surprise. Gérard LeBlond abandoned his score and rushed to my father's side. And the organ stopped playing.

Montreal, PQ

THE PASTOR of Thetford Mines left town in a hearse. He was driven to Dorval Airport, slipped into a sealed casket, and loaded onto a Swissair flight bound for Copenhagen, via Geneva. In Denmark, another appropriate vehicle drove him to Skagen, where, with his family in attendance, carrying his binoculars and the six-flapped cap I had coiffed him with, he disappeared into the earth, buried in the sands of his cemetery whipped by the fury of the winds.

I had informed my mother, and she made the trip. The family welcomed her as in the best of times. When Johanes' casket was lowered into the ground to the sound of the old church bells, she produced a small square of paper towel and dabbed at the corner of one eye that was as dry as a bone. She touched my shoulder and spoke a few words, keeping the distance she had always maintained. It was like being in the company of a vague relation, a maiden aunt, and conjuring up an old friend whose day had come. There was no more father or mother, no more child, only two adults walking among the tombs and remembering the death of a third who had once been familiar, and was now the inevitable collateral damage of passing time.

My mother did not know what the last two years of Johanes' life had been like, and neither did the Hansen family. There was no reason for them to find out. She went back to Geneva, and the others returned to their fish. And I moved off towards what I hoped would be a second new life.

At the request of the United Church Presbytery, no service nor ceremony was organised in memory of Pastor Hansen. The accounts, both ecclesiastical and financial, were definitively closed on his debts, and the faithful changed parishes as they waited for another minister to be named. Gérard, out of love for the instrument but also in memory of my father, purchased the Hammond B3, with its pedalboard and Leslie speaker. The diocese did not have to be asked twice. Who knows, perhaps the speaker, somewhere in the vicinity of Sherbrooke, is still blasting out gusts of chords, sevenths and ninths. For a number of years, Gérard LeBlond and I – I had moved to Montreal by then – stayed in touch by phone, and related to one another the uneven progress of our respective lives. He told me that the new pastor hired to replace Johanes attracted only a handful of customers from another era. The faithful, who, as he put it, "would have attended even if there'd been a raccoon in the pulpit". A few years later, Gérard called me at eleven at night. He was that eager to reveal what he had learned. The Thetford Mines church had been closed a year earlier, once the English-speaking parishioners had deserted it. It was sold, just as my mother's movie theatre had been. The real estate agent had found a buyer, who took the parish house as well, and turned it into an apartment complex. "If your father saw that, believe me, he wouldn't have regretted the afternoons he spent at the racetrack. One of these days I'm going to go have a look, and I'll tell you what it's like." I did not hear from Gérard again – I think I know why – and I never returned to Thetford Mines. I only hope that the new tenants kept the vault and the ribs of their new ship, where once the sound of my father's voice echoed.

After his death, I left my job with DuLaurier. He threw me a little goodbye party. To mark the occasion, as if he knew what my future held, Pierre gave me a very well-stocked tool-box, filled with an array of powerful instruments for sawing, sanding, plating, drilling and hammering. "I don't know what you're going to do next, but with all this hardware, and what you learned with us, you'll be able to make a living and find your way. Good luck, son." No-one had called me son in a very long time. I packed my new tools and the few possessions I owned into the three and a half square metres of my Honda, which was as light as a feather, then set sights on the city, steady as she goes, destination Montreal, PQ.

In prison, we avoid confiding in each other and rarely speak of our families. Patrick told me about his a few times, and I was quick to understand that relating his younger years was a source of pain. I never revealed much either. When it came to my mother, all I told him was that she was a very modern, combative and spectacularly beautiful woman. "Hey, that's your mother. You don't talk about your mother like that, fuck, it doesn't sound right. Spectacularly beautiful – it's like you're talking about a barmaid on the strip. When you say that, sorry, but you don't want to know the pictures going around inside my head. No, man, your mother is your mother, and that's that."

Another time, I let on that my father was Danish, and a pastor until his death. Patrick quickly made me see my mistake. "Shit, you're a minister's son. Too much! Pretty weird if you ask me. What did your old man do all day? I mean, the mass and all the rest, that only takes up Sunday. I can't imagine what that would be like, being the son of a kind of a priest, weird. And the minister lived with the spectacular beauty? That doesn't add up, man. I know that ministers are allowed to do it, but, fuck, with your mother, the way you talk about her, that's just too weird for words. Sorry, but us Catholics aren't used to that. In our church, fucking's not allowed. The priests aren't supposed to. They can't even wax their weasels now and then. Officially, that is. So your father was doing it with your spectacular mother just before going off to church, sorry, man, but I just don't see it." We never got past that point. Family episodes and the comparative merits of Papist versus Huguenot practices were banished from our cohabitation.

Today, Patrick is looking nervous. He got a letter from his unspectacular mother announcing she was coming to visit him this afternoon in the usual room. For the occasion, he shaved and went hunting for some clothes that were not too wrinkled, rare items in a cell like ours, managed by two men and a half. I watched as he carefully combed his hair, a first since we started living together. He was like a teenager going on his first date. His nervous anticipation began the moment her letter was delivered. He immediately turned into the son of the teacher who liked other people's children and who threatened him with a beating if he left his hockey stick in the hall, and his mother whom he hardly ever sees. In some way, he understands that his mother loved him, even if she never showed it. Otherwise, why would she travel so far, to this infamous prison with its foul visiting room? Of course she loved him, even when he misbehaved and the teacher tanned his hide in his room. She did not defend him because he was not defendable, and besides, her husband would not have allowed it. Secretly, she waited for him to disappear so she could begin living again, and take each of her children in her arms and ask their forgiveness. "Does this brown shirt go with my blue pants, or do I wear the grey one? I've been inside so long I don't know how to dress." He hesitates. He wonders what Mama will think. If she will judge his appearance or take him as he is, a violent man of no account, but the fruit of her loins all the same, the result of a quickie and a squirt of teacher juice, one night when he took it into his mind. Patrick is enormously touching. I hope she will treat him well.

I moved to Montreal around the time I received my invitation to the official ceremony to mark the swearing in. After five years of waiting, I was becoming a Canadian citizen. A hundred people from all around the globe came together in a special hall with two Canadian flags, a member of the Mounted Police in dress uniform, a citizenship judge in robes, and a clerk of the court wearing a series of gold chains. A certificate was presented to each individual with the same warm words: "Welcome to the great Canadian family." Then everyone stood up to sing "O Canada", the national anthem written by Calixa Lavallée, with words by Adolphe-Basile Routhier.

I crossed Jeanne-Mance Park and walked down Saint Urbain to the Place des Arts, and ordered a hot chocolate at Café 87. Nothing had changed, except that I was a Canadian now. With my new certificate in my pocket, I could claim the status of Franco-Canadian, in addition to being the son of a Dane from Skagen. I had signed a new lease on a territory; it was the first time I had chosen my dwelling place. It was quite a different experience. As for the anthem "O Canada", it was a mixture of the worst religious and military metaphors: "God keep our land glorious and free! / O Canada we stand on guard for thee." The simplest of rhythms and rhymes hammered out between two steins of beer, it wasn't much better than the dreadful, terrifying "Marseillaise" of my native land. I know that any self-respecting Franco-Canadian who longs for a little peace and dignity on this earth should never think – let alone say – what I am going to write next. When it comes to national anthems, nothing can beat, wherever it is played and whatever the reason, "God Save the Queen". Every time I hear it, I regret not being born British.

I liked Montreal. It was a car-friendly city, a comfortable place, one of the rare ones in this world that can smooth out the jolts and shocks of life, and absorb and ease the pain life sometimes brings. The mountain, the fountains, the parks, the river, the humming of the human hive rushing off to its disparate tasks, and slowly, in the evening, dispersing towards the luminous alveoli of its great apartment buildings. I had no trouble blending into the crowd, first as a clerk in a Rona hardware store on Notre-Dame Street, a veritable paradise of tools and accessories, with aisles cutting their way through shelves that reached the sky and that were loaded with the most improbable freight. Then over to Loblaw's, a supermarket chain that sold more than food, where I was asked to stock the fruit and vegetable section with products that seemed to have been varnished. And after that, the Canadian Tire on Saint Lawrence Boulevard, a purveyor of automotive equipment and supplier of common repairs for most models. For almost a year, in my bay in the garage, I replaced filters and sparkplugs, and changed the oil on everything on wheels, as the slogan ran. Eight vehicles a day. Nearly one hundred and sixty a month. Some one thousand, six hundred in a year.

Lubricating is not a vocation. No-one can spend his days discoursing on the viscosity of Valvoline, Pennzoil, Quaker State, Castrol, Royal Purple and Amsoil. I discovered, in this area, that there really is a category of obsessive customers who maintain strange, almost emotional relations with their lubricants. These men, over the course of their lives, displayed greater fidelity to those plastic bottles of refined petroleum products spiked with additives than to the spouses who had the patience to watch them grow old and listen to them make the same old complaints about cars that burn more oil than they should.

I left the world of oil and tyres eight days before my thirtieth birthday. I was living in a one-bedroom apartment on Clark Street, on the edge of Little Italy, down from Jarry Park.

The building superintendent was surely one of the strangest and funniest men in the city, and my friendly feelings for him knew no bounds. During working hours, no matter the season, he wore the same thing: steel-toed shoes, high woollen socks, Bermuda shorts with reinforced side pockets, a black sweatshirt and a chocolate-brown jacket with UPS stamped on it. Was his life's dream to criss-cross the city for this delivery company? Perhaps, since he sported its coat of arms and characteristic suit proudly. When he was on duty in the building, he imitated the sounds of modern domestic life to perfection. He vibrated like a blender as he cleaned the front door, washed the windows while imitating the vacuum cleaner that he would run to the sound of a Formula 1 engine going through its gears, making the well-lubricated doors squeak. When evening fell and it was time to light a cigarette out on the front steps of the building, he imitated the sound of a fishing boat's diesel engine as it pulled out of port. During these performances, Sergei Bubka was alone in his world, trying neither to please nor entertain. When he pushed off from the shore, with the tide just right, he stood alone at the wheel of his trawler, comforted by the hum of the Perkins engine. In a way all his own, he created his own world, and made a soundtrack for his dreams the way children do with their motorised mouths as they push their Dinky Toys along the highways of the living room. I got along very well with Sergei Bubka. When I returned home, he was sometimes in the lobby. "What do you want this time?" he would ask. And I would make my request. "The subway doors opening and closing." A moment later, the signal sounded and I stepped into the car. It was that simple.

I owe Bubka so much. He is the one who ushered me into my new life. This time, without so much as imitating the sound of the handshake that seals the deal, he introduced me to Noël Alexandre, the president of the condo owners' association for the Excelsior building, in the Ahuntsic district, not far from the park of the same name. From time to time I fixed small electrical or plumbing problems that had stumped Sergei, which earned me his admiration and eternal gratitude. So when Alexandre, who once lived in this building, let on during a chance meeting that he was looking for a new superintendent to replace the current one who was not working out, Bubka told him right out, "I have the man you need." "Do you know what Mr Alexandre said to me? Send him right over! Then he asked, 'Does he make noises like you?' I like Mr Alexandre, he's a very respectful fellow."

A month later, I moved into the Excelsior, a great ocean liner of a building, with its machine room, complex inner workings, an Olympic swimming pool, a luxurious garden and sixty-eight cabins spread over six decks. One on the ground floor, no doubt the least desirable, was reserved for me. I was taken on as the janitor with the promise of an upgrade to superintendent if, after three years, I proved satisfactory. Instead of putting on the uniform of a ship's captain, I slipped into the khaki monkey suit of the Excelsior jack-of-all-trades.

My first year was one long nightmare. I had to battle fatigue, discouragement, dark shadows. Overrun by ongoing tasks, individual demands, system breakdowns, ordinary maintenance multiplied by the harsh winters, I almost quit any number of times. I lost nine kilos during that first period.

And my sleep, one night out of two. The belly of the beast was my home. Even after six months, I still could not put a name to the faces of the residents when I crossed paths with them in the common areas.

Patrick was completely right to scoff at my father's schedule. When it came to intensity, concentration, sheer work and fatigue, running a church – making it go smoothly, balancing the wattage of the Leslie and straightening the bent parts of the English congregation once a week – truly was a lark, a leisure activity, a hobby. When I think about it, I never once remember my father complaining, except during his period of chasing horses and crap tables. The long hours of driving through the night, the anxieties as his losses grew, the fear that his double life would come to light did wear on him. But before, during all those years when the pew-sitters hovered near, I always knew him to be vigorous and energetic, as fresh as a daisy.

At the Excelsior, rosebushes with thorns as jagged as daggers awaited me in the garden, and I had to treat and trim them at the right time of year, cutting diagonally, leaving three buds on the weaker branches. Then bundle them up for winter. And see to the elder trees, the shadberries, the Himalayan blue cedar, the hydrangea, rake up the autumn leaves dropped by the ton by a maple grove. And the lawn, always thirsty during the summer, which had to be kept impeccably green, and cut short but not scalped. And the swimming pool, in which I drowned more than once, unable to maintain the equilibrium of the two hundred and thirty thousand litres of water just waiting to go sour when their pH dropped too low, either that or they performed some biological eccentricity such as inviting in a colony of algae that, according to their shape and form, would turn the pool into a giant milk bath, or give it the unpleasant hue of spinach. Before salt was used to treat the pool, I fought the best I could with quadruple-action chlorine, pH+, and bottles of liquid flocculants to drive all the crap to the bottom, where I could then vacuum it up and send it down the sewer. Besides the indecently high cost of the operation, it took for ever, under the strict and impatient surveillance of the owners strapped into their swimsuits. These microorganisms devoured my life and sometimes forced me into bedside visits to the pool in the middle of the night to evaluate the damage, before the owners could wake up and discover the situation. Up until the day when these waters were finally treated with salt and uniformly kept at twenty-eight degrees from the end of April to mid-October, using electric heat during the swimming season, I cohabited with those two hundred and thirty thousand litres of water that hung over my head like a sword in the night, apt, at any moment, to renounce our treaty and drown me in shame.

More than once I had to knock on Noël Alexandre's door and confess my failure, assuming the crestfallen posture of the contrite clerk. "It got away on me last night." Alexandre would turn to his wife. "It got away on us last night." Less than an hour later, everyone was standing on their balcony, eyes glued to the disaster, repeating, yes, of course, it got away on us last night.

The pool was long a source of worry and endless unpleasantness. All the more curious, because it was also, many years later, at the origin of my being fired and, as a consequence, my imprisonment. But that time, the motives had nothing to do with the reaction of hydrogen compounds.

Even worse, the complications surrounding this body of water did not disappear when the season turned cold. When autumn arrived, the pool had to be emptied, and the two hundred and thirty cubic metres of its contents were flushed into the sewer so that, in the dead of winter, the cold temperatures would not cause the concrete and the pipes to break apart. Although it was a necessary operation, I could never begin the protocol without a sharp sense of shame and the feeling I was committing an evil act. I thought of the two hundred and thirty thousand litres treated with chlorine, then later on, with special salts, heated to the desired temperature for six months so that the majority of the residents could practise their over-arm stroke without shivering. And then, I pulled the plug and sent the pure waters of this small urban ocean into the nether-world of the sewer system.

The second phase of the hibernation process used an air compressor to bleed the filtration units, both upper and lower, and the evacuation system, then shut down the heat. Finally, I could wait for the snow to cast a blanket of amnesia over this blue void until the following year.

From my early experiences, I learned one simple lesson. Apartment buildings often resemble the people who live in them, and those people like it that way.

There is an infinite number of ways to ruin your existence. My grandfather chose a Citroën DS 19. My father, the clergy. I preferred to enter this secular monastery that wrapped the days of my life in the cotton batting of routine. Outside unexpected breakdowns and emergencies, my schedule was always the same. In the morning, I would conduct my rounds in the hallways and check on the general cleanliness of the place. Then I tested the lifts, the lighting, the electrical systems, and, no matter the weather or the temperature, I climbed up to the roof to see how the ventilation was functioning. Eight stacks, each equipped with three motors designed for maximum output, odour extraction and dehumidifying. I made sure the flow-back valves were working and paid close attention to the noise each group made as it functioned, listening for the first complaints of a worn piece of equipment. Once back inside, I journeyed to the basement to test the motor on the sump pump, grease the moving panels of the garage door and check the fire alarm system, as well as the security apparatus that allowed access to the building through magnetic badges. Once that was behind me, my day of maintenance could finally begin. I stopped in the room where the recording equipment was stored, to which the twenty-four surveillance cameras covering most of the building's interior and exterior sent their images.

That preliminary inspection was necessary. It helped me anticipate problems before they had a chance to create a waterfall of further dysfunction.

The Excelsior was made in the image of its swimming pool. A fragile building, but full of fantasy, playful, ready to kick up its heels. No matter the season, I had to keep an eye on it. Otherwise, if I looked the other way, it would throw me off like a bucking bronco. Then I would have to work like the devil to make it behave reasonably again. The Excelsior was like toothpaste. Always eager to squirt out of its tube, and not so easy to get back in again.

Two days ago, an epidemic of gastroenteritis broke out, and it spared no part of the prison. It was truly torture, and the promiscuity and shared toilets contributed to spreading the disease. The cells fell one after the other, and the Imodium rations do not seem to be having an effect so far. The stink of the plague floats through every wing. The guards wear masks and latex gloves, and have been ordered not to have any contact with the inmates. I was hoping the disease would pass over our condo, but yesterday it was our turn to fall victim to it. People blame the food for the lightning-fast spread of the sickness. To have to sit face to face with someone and empty your guts in a state of emergency is devastatingly humiliating. No-one is born to live through that. The violence of this world and its brutality is something that I just cannot accept. Every time I have to go, I rush for the toilet and ask Patrick to excuse me. "Don't be such a little girl, man. That's the way it is. They've got us where they want us. So don't complicate things. Just get rid of it, relieve yourself, and don't pay any attention to me. I don't see anything, I don't hear anything, I don't smell anything. Get it?"

There is something almost noble in Patrick's animal savagery, something that places him above his judges and guards, above his father, who spent his life teaching, but who learned nothing. Just when I least expect it, when the situation does not lend itself, he sends out a flash of light, a quick stroke of humanity.

A guard told us that everything would be back to normal in a week, according to the doctor. In the meantime, we would be eating rice. Patrick and I try to sleep as much as possible, but our guts revolt in noisy spasms, reminding us who's boss. Before he went to bed, he made a request. "If we're better, could you cut my hair tomorrow?" He must really trust me if he asked me to do that job. Anyone who has ever witnessed a session of capillary beautification by this particular animal, even once, would demand a transfer to another cell, even with the round-nosed tool that is allowed in here.

And things are better this morning. The odour seems to have migrated elsewhere in the night and our guts obey us. Patrick is ready. He sits on the stool, a towel over his shoulders, his back straight. Tense and anxious to the extreme. His jaw is so painfully set and his throat so tight he can scarcely give me the directions he has in mind. "Not too short, right, and cut little by little, no big clumps of hair. I don't want to hear the sound of the scissors running through my hair. So take it easy. If I don't feel good, I'll tell you and you'll stop. If I really don't feel good, I'll have to lie down on the floor. That's normal, don't worry. I trust you. Look, give me another minute or two and then we'll start."

Patrick Horton suffers from a phobia that has dogged him since childhood. He believes that his hair is an integral part of his body, and having it cut triggers definite physical symptoms. "I don't know how to describe it. It's like if you cut off a part of my finger or a little piece of my ear. Like you amputated some part of me. The pain is too much. My hair is a complete part of me. That's why I can't go to the barber's. Back home, my mother would cut it. She knew how to do it, she talked to me, the whole thing. I can't do it myself. I tried using the mirror, but every time I closed the scissors I started to faint. Can you imagine cutting off the tip of your own tongue?"

I run my hand through Patrick's hair. With infinite care, I begin to snip away, one strand at a time, at his tangled head. I might as well be slashing my way through the jungle with nail clippers. "Go easy, not too much at a time, and don't pull. And don't make my hair crack, I can't stand that sound." Patrick's body begins to tremble softly, and pearls of anxiety bloom on his upper lip. "Stop, OK, stop. I need a break for a couple minutes." On the floor, not a heap or a mound, just a suggestion of hair. At this rate, it will take a week. During the time out, I make us a cup of coffee, and Patrick drinks it, shivering, both hands around the mug, like a shipwrecked sailor freshly rescued from the reef.

The scissors do their best, but even when they work slowly, their blades make the characteristic high-pitched sound as they nibble at the cuticle, the cortex, the medulla. And that is exactly what Patrick cannot stand. "Stop, fuck, I can't take it, my head's spinning, I've got to lie down, fuck." The man and a half gently slips off his stool and onto the floor, curling up in a ball like a large tame animal. I squat down next to him and put my hand on his shoulder. I listen to his breathing as it slowly grows calmer, and we stay like that, side by side, for as long as it takes.

. . .

My panicked nights and crises of confidence lessened with time, and with the passing years, the Excelsior's timorous janitor, according to the clauses of the agreement and after a third term, was promoted to the level of general superintendent. To put it more baldly, my new status was accompanied by a raise, but more importantly, a higher level of responsibilities, since the administrative management of the building was added to my tasks. It was my job to purchase the consumables, order products and tools for maintenance, work with the companies that were employed by the Excelsior, and make the necessary appointments. In other words, I was running a small business. Once I adapted to the new conditions, I slipped easily into the superintendent's skin. People called me by my first name. I became the building's lynchpin, and little by little its familiar, even its confidant.

My theatre of action stopped at the door of each apartment. What occurred beyond that point did not concern me. The owners had to deal with their equipment failures, leaks, blackouts, phone bugs and cable issues.

In the early 1990s, the Excelsior featured an older population who had settled there at the very beginning with the goal of living out their retirement there when the time came, in a comfortable, distinguished setting. And now that time had come. Lady Luck had decided to spoil the owners, and she found them a Franco-Canadian superintendent with no special qualifications, but who specialised in everything, and could make short work of breakdowns, leaks, blackouts, telephone snafus and twisted cables. Though the rules prohibited it, every door of every hallway opened to me. I stepped forth from my apartment; the entire building became my secondary residence. During those years, of the sixty-eight apartments, twenty-one were occupied by women on their own, and rather aged, too. All of them counted on me. To unblock a sink, or conjure up the past, perhaps even lighten a memory about to overflow. Some evenings, I felt as though I had spent more time listening to the creak of old souls than checking on the squeaking extractors on the roof. I was thirty-five years old, had the patience of an angel, and one desire that would never leave me, that of wanting to repair things, treat them well, care for them, keep watch over them. If requested to, why not act the same way with the sixty-eight owners, whose motto was: "If you have a problem, Paul has the solution."

On May 14, 1991, I was confronted by a problem with no solution. Gunther Ganz, my mother's companion, called me in the middle of the night to inform me she was dead.

I can still hear his big barrel of a voice shot through with a German accent telling me over the phone, "Your mother died an hour ago. She did not suffer. It was suicide."

Dorval Airport. An Air Canada flight. Seven and a half hours, overnight to Geneva Cointrin. Ganz waiting for me. A Mercedes from the 1970s. A man of few words. The dark interior of the house, full of the past. The staircase covered in red velvet, the wood creaking underneath. The bedroom, my mother's body. Dressed for an evening out. Her hands crossed over her stomach. Her face repainted with the colours of life. As if she were resting. Death had paid a quick visit, then moved on. When she opened her eyes, she would see her son and ask him to sit by her side. She was wearing no watch, no jewellery. Ganz had stored everything in a safe. He loved to tidy things up. I wanted to hold my mother's hands in mine, and touch her face, but I didn't dare. Ganz stood beside me, looking like a sceptical customs agent. A motorcycle went by outside. In the distance, a cove, part of the lake.

"The cremation is tomorrow morning." On the night table, the vials were still there. In a row, lined up like a small triumphant army. "It was suicide."

He had told me as much twice, once over the phone, and again at the airport. I am this woman's son. I look after a building. I help old people, some of them are sick. I, too, would like to bring back the dead. I sat on the edge of the bed, I stroked her skin, and it was as cold as my father's. And then, very far from Ganz, an infinitesimal spectre, carrying all the silt of our lives, returning along the paths of childhood, filled with a first love that was still intact, bearing the many things we would never have again, the tears of little Paul Hansen fell upon the cottony sleeve of my mother's gown.

Ganz, the Swiss Guard of eternity, the contraband fakir, held his pose. The motorcycle went back the other way.

The Saint-Georges Crematorium, chemin de la Bâtie, in Geneva. Conifers, wide stairways leading to a big block of cement and glass. Aborted turrets rose above the roof. The big BBC ovens tiled with white ceramic. "Your mother refused the religious service." Ganz with his voice of the damned, feeling obliged to state the obvious. I figured the ex-wife of the horse-loving pastor, Anna Margerit, my mother, former *Deep Throat* ambassadress, preacher of *Pigsty*, atheist by birth, was not going to go begging for Christian unction before heading off to burn in the gas oven. Like Medea, she would enter hell impious, bringing with her all the grace and beauty the world contained.

The return trip dissolved into a weary half-sleep. When I arrived, the sun was casting rays of beauty upon Dorval, Canada looked like Mallorca, the Excelsior was sunning itself poolside, its water immaculate. Despite the late hour, I went up on the roof to check the ventilation and make sure my little world was breathing freely and still turning as it should, in serene silence, without the slightest friction.

Winona's Wings

PATRICK'S CAPILLARY ADVENTURES halted there. He decided to keep every follicle of his skull covering and wrap it in a sort of black headscarf, the kind that some African Americans used to wear when they had their hair straightened. Today, the prison is hopping. An official from the Ministry of Justice is coming to tour our house of detention. When he is present, all cell doors must remain open, with the prisoners inside. The Ministry's representative will visit each wing and engage in dialogue with the inmates.

The news has cheered up Patrick. When he heard about the visit, he began composing a little notebook of complaints, the contents of which only he knows. He intends to give it to our visitor if he stops off at our cell.

Like a great bear emerging after a long winter, Patrick Horton has recovered his vigour. A potential meeting with a member of the government department that concerns him is the equivalent of a big pot of honey, sharpening his appetite.

Richard Sorel timidly knocked upon our door. Flanked by two members of the Quebec Provincial Police, he entered and presented us, Patrick and me, with his bona fides. Sorel looked like a fine enough human being. There was no denying that. He was probably the last or next to last of a standard family of twelve or thirteen children that his father had to run herd on for an interminable number of years, and you could tell that at mealtimes all the others ate before he did. Which explained why, even as an adult, he continued to look so skinny that his shirt floated around his neck like a lifejacket. Patrick stared at Richard Sorel, almost intimidated by such a frail being, disappointed that he could not assert his rights with a solid piece of work from his usual world. When the Deputy Minister asked if we had any observations to make about Bordeaux Prison, Patrick took the floor. "I wrote you a little list on this paper, but before that, I am going to clear up a few things. First of all, unlike the rest, I shouldn't be here. I'm innocent. All the accusations are false. I'm a member of the Hell's Angels, that's true, but I'm only interested in motorcycles, and the other stuff, the drugs and all that, I never touch it. That's the first point. Now I'm going to ask you two or three questions. I don't know where you live, but could you live here, in this tiny box, twenty-four hours a day, with a guy you never met before you ended up in Bordeaux? Eat and sleep every night with him? Shit in front of him? Because that's what it's called. Three hundred days a year, we eat boiled chicken with some kind of crap, you don't even know what it is. Not only is the grub lousy, it's dangerous. You can ask anyone, they'll tell you. Last week we all caught the runs, the whole place all at once, all of us shitting our guts out day and night in front of everyone else and eating Imodium by the handful. What about rats and mice, you have them at your place? They live here with us permanently, scratching away every night. A hell of a noise that keeps you from sleeping. We have to plug up the openings with steel and nails. Oh, I forgot about the heating. I don't know what the weather was in your office at Christmas, but here, this winter, we slept in our clothes, all wrapped up in blankets that stank of old tyres. And I'll skip the rest, the exercise yard that's been cut back, the so-called activities, and the guards that treat us like shit. So imagine all that when you're innocent. If you want more information, I put my name on the paper. Horton. Patrick Horton."

In the backpack that served as his suit, and the clothes that traced out his bony frame, Deputy Minister Sorel looked as though he had just stepped out of a dryer. And that was just about what had happened. He had encountered the man and a half in tip-top shape, pugnacious, full of details and concise. Sorel would need some time to get his wits about him again.

Before he left our cell with the two policemen whose presence made our little condo feel even smaller, Richard Sorel offered me his hand, full of what I wasn't sure, then turned and spoke to Patrick. "I appreciate your courage and your honest words." Then the skinny little guy went out the way he came in, discreetly, out the door, flanked by his QPP guards.

That evening the warden came visiting to see if all had gone well with the Ministry representative. "I hope you didn't talk too much nonsense, Horton." Slipping his headscarf back on his scalp, Patrick smiled. "Me, talk nonsense, chief? Never."

. . .

At the very beginning of June 1991, in the meeting room, the plenary of the Excelsior's Annual General Meeting took place, presided over by my benefactor, Noël Alexandre. Nearly every owner attended the event at which the priority expenditures of the coming year were decided upon, and the past year's budget examined and approved. It was like a family gathering with, at times, its share of friction, but when all was said and done, everyone raised a glass of bubbly together, or a goblet of fruity Chardonnay.

Kieran Read, who for once was not travelling for work, attended the statutory celebrations, greeting the other residents with a smile and a nod, without getting too friendly. I remember very well how we chatted that evening about a business trip that had taken him to Baltimore. A sordid story. Four children had teamed up with the insurance company to reveal the private moral turpitude of their late father, so that the very large benefit paid to their mother would be cut down to a scandalously low figure. "My job, unfortunately, was to record their testimony – that was why I was called. I never understood why they sullied their father's name and impoverished their mother like that. The way I figured it, the insurance company must have shown its gratitude to the ungrateful children by paying each of them a little extra. From what I understand, Paul, you don't have children. Good, keep it that way. Believe me, sooner or later they end up fouling the nest."

When he returned from certain missions that, from the human point of view, were extremely trying, Kieran often had a low opinion of himself and his fellows. He would retreat into his apartment for several days, in need of decontamination before going back to his normal life, which would begin with the next call from the company. "You know, casualties adjuster is no kind of trade to have. I started out as a lawyer working essentially with the unions. Then my mother fell ill. Between the treatment and the operations, she lost all her savings in six months. Our health insurance paid for most of it, but I had to help out with the rest, long-term care and specialised personnel. That's when I was offered my first job. I remember it well. A strange story. The victim was driving along in his pickup truck at 100 kilometres an hour down a country road. As he was taking a curve, a horse appeared out of nowhere, right in front of him. He hit the animal, and it flew through the windshield and went out the back window. Hard to believe, but that's exactly what happened. When help arrived, the ambulance attendants found the driver had been completely crushed by the animal as it passed through the inside of the truck. That was my introduction to the business. It happened not too far from here, in upstate New York. I was taken on to enquire into the dead man's past. Thanks to careless horses and unlucky men, I was able to offer my mother a decent life for another seven or eight years. Do you still have your parents, Paul?"

A couple of weeks earlier, I could have said yes. But now, today, no, both my parents were dead. There was no reason to enquire into anything. Neither of them had crossed paths with a horse. Except maybe my father, with his binoculars and cap, on the home stretch.

As time passed, it became clearer to me that with each year Kieran was bending ever lower under the weight of those dead people whose pockets he had to search. Always at the epicentre of tragedy, dealing with insurance companies ready to do anything to cut back their payouts, families eager to bump up their benefits, unpredictable judges and lawyers ferocious when it came to the cost of the advice they doled out, he stewed in this deleterious cauldron of humanity where the worst sins simmered, with the lowest cuts of the species. His job was to avoid a trial at all costs, and to that end, he thwarted the victim's parents, negotiated on the side, letting them believe the company was on their side, displaying compassion during these difficult times, convincing them to accept his offer, smaller than their expectations, perhaps, but available now, immediately, avoiding a long trial whose outcome was uncertain, with its inquiries and counter-inquiries into their private lives and the enormous lawyers' fees. That was how the adjuster, in the privacy of a living room, lowered payouts to people weakened by mourning and worried about what might be found in the father's pockets, or in his closet.

Shortly after the condo owners' meeting, he knocked at my door. "Are you doing something special, Paul? If you don't mind, I'll take you out to dinner. I spent all day reading a file, I can't take it anymore, my head is about to explode from the nastiness."

When we pushed our way through the Excelsior doors at 1.30 in the morning, Kieran Read, holding on to my arm, was talking a mile a minute, jettisoning everything that burdened him and sullied his memory, throwing off his shame and regret in the neutral atmosphere of our lobby, which sparkled with mirrors and halogen lighting. "Really, none of it is very complicated. Actually, it's very simple. Life's inequalities are generally reinforced and confirmed in the halls of justice, and that is true until our dying day. For an insurance company, the death of a New York business executive is a regrettable mess, because the indemnity paid to the family will be between ten and twenty times higher than the sum offered to a horse farmer who went missing in Montana. There is a cartography of misfortune, everyone knows that, a list of counties where a dead man is worth his weight in gold. You know what the worst case is for an insurance company that can't come to an agreement with the victim's family, and that ends up in court? No need to scratch your head. A child killed by an airbag, or a forty-year-old white male, living in a city, with a good job, married, two kids, loves his family, takes care of his aged parents. In both cases, it's ruination for the company. When the case looks too good, like the forty-year-old white guy, that's when they call me in to investigate. About his health, for example. It's weird, but a dead person's health can influence the amount of the indemnity. A smoker can have his value go down. Someone treated for hypertension – even worse. HIV positive, forget about it. When it comes to the scales that are applied in the profession, and for juries, a victim who was sociable, went out with his friends, was athletic, an outdoorsy person, that guy is worth more than someone who didn't have many friends, who stayed home and read or watched TV. America is this wonderful place, this marvellous territory where people want their dead to be athletic, active and above all in good health. And don't forget the supplementary amount for the family of the dear departed who practised what we call 'loyal family sexuality'. In court, the widow just has to declare that she has been deprived of 'satisfying and frequent sexual relations' and the jury will lubricate her grief with an extra 250 to 300 thousand dollars. And you know what, Paul? Strange but true, it's been documented every time: the prettier the widow, the higher the compensation. If a housewife dies in an accident, a domestic expert is named to evaluate, beyond the *pretium doloris*, the indemnity awarded to compensate the sum of domestic and family work the woman carried out in her home. Cooking, cleaning, errands, raising the children, running the family budget. All that will be weighed and evaluated at market value and a figure assigned for 'economic losses'. These days, the amounts requested for pain and suffering and emotional loss, when large insurance firms are involved, have reached the most outlandish figures. In a case that was recently judged, *Qualls* v. *Case*, I remember it well, the office of Booth and Koskoff in the Los Angeles area, which represented the claimant, picked up 17.5 million dollars. But before they dip into petty cash, the companies ask us to sniff around and scratch at the surface, and check to see whether the dead man had a taste for pleasure, and maybe jumped the fence from time to time. That's how it works, Paul, exactly that way. I do a dirty job with dirty methods, surrounded by dirty people. When you die, even if things in Canada are a little different, your actual posthumous value might well depend on the vice of a lawyer or the virtue of an adjuster, the past you had, the future you won't have, the colour of your skin, your bad luck and your abilities when it came to a 'satisfying and frequent' sex life. Satisfying and frequent, Paul, don't forget that as long as you live."

I asked Kieran why, after his mother's death, he simply did not drop the business, and consign that world to the dust heap, and go back to his original trade. He told me it was too late, he did not have the courage to start all over again. He had taken the wrong turn and he knew it, but he would stick to that path until the end. That night, I had all the trouble in the world falling asleep. It was Kieran's fault: the confessions that made me feel queasy, certain of his stories that rattled around in my head, even after he left my place. That night, a man and a woman were speeding along in their car. A trac-tor trailer coming from the right pulled out directly in front of them. They did not even have time to hit the brakes. They drove right under the trailer that sliced off the top part of their car. When it was all over, the car came to a stop a hundred metres further on. Upright, strapped into their seats, the bod-ies of the man and woman. Their skulls had been split open at the exact same spot, leaving only the jawbone and the lower teeth of each victim. The upper part of their heads was spread across the road, hair and brains tangled together. What was the veritable state of their health? Were they outdoorsy people, frequently satisfied?

This morning, the world had better give Patrick a wide berth. His lawyer informed him that his motorcycle could well be seized by the court as evidence in his case. More to the point, his Fat Boy with a Milwaukee-Eight 107 engine, six speeds, valued at 25 thousand dollars, 1,745 cubic centimetres, which works out at $14.32 per cc. A photo of the Fat Boy is displayed on his shelf in our cell. I would like to have the chance to tell the judge not to lay hands on the bike, for that would surely awaken the volcano, and the man and a half would turn into more than two. I would like to have the chance to tell the judge that whatever Patrick did, whatever act he committed, the bike must be left at the very spot it is parked, no-one must lay so much as a hand on it, let the Fat Boy sleep beneath its sheet of plastic, sheltered from time and the justice of men. If anything can save Patrick Horton, it will be his Harley and its cubic centimetres at $14.32 a piece. Seizing the bike would mean starting a conflict, declaring war on Patrick, running the risk of destroying whatever humanity remains. And turning him into the next Maurice "Mom" Boucher, the former leader of the Hell's Angels, sentenced to prison for life for the murder of two guards.

All morning, Patrick paced and muttered to himself. "Anyone touch my bike, he's dead, fuck, I'll bust his ass. I swear, I'll break every bone in his body." He was not talking to anyone in particular, he stomped and growled out his rage like a wild animal whose prey has been snatched away from him. Around noon, intrigued by his mood, two guards came to talk to him in the corridor. They had a little chat. Two hours later, he was escorted to the warden's office.

Emmanuel Savage is no worse than any other man. Like everyone else, he is doing a dirty job surrounded by a bunch of dirty guys who, for the most part, have led dirty lives up to now. He runs this wreck of an establishment with what the Ministry provides him to house and feed his roomers. He drops in on us now and then. He does not bother putting on airs, no excessive severity, no overflowing empathy either. That is about all I can say about the man who took less than two hours to summon Patrick to his office once he learned that the prisoner wanted to kick the shit out of a quarter of the population of the west end of town.

In the middle of the afternoon, I saw Patrick coming down the corridor with that particular gait he has when things are going well, and he is happy to be alive. At times like that, he seems to be wearing shoes mounted on springs that push him skywards with every step. His face shines, and like a young politician on the stump, he smiles and waves at every man he meets. When he came into the cell, he had no eyes for me. He went straight to the photo of his Fat Boy and kissed it as if it were his son back from the war. "Savage is too much, really. Can you believe it? He invites me up to see him, asks me what the hell is going on and why I'm spreading shit. I explain what the trouble is, I get right to the point, he nods and tells me, 'Wait outside, I'll call the clerk.' Five minutes later, not even, he tells me, 'Alright, it's settled, the Fat Boy stays at your place. Your lawyer got it all wrong. So you can stop bugging us.' And then, instead of throwing me out, he sits me down, that's right, Savage sits me down, and you know what? He starts talking bikes, and I can tell the guy is really into it. He asks me about the Fat Boy, the kind of questions that a guy who drives an Audi would never think of. Then he cuts to the chase and tells me that he has a Harley, too, a Softail Slim, you don't know what that is, but it's a real hard-ass bike, a piece of quality engineering that sits on a crazy set of tyres, 150/80B1677H in back, a little smaller in front. Can you feature that, the boss, Savage himself, cruising on a Softail? Shit, when he told me that it was alright for my bike, I could have Frenched him. And then, all that business about his Slim and the rubber it rolls on, can you believe it, it was pure gold. Try and imagine it! The boss on a Harley! Sorry, sonny boy, if you don't mind, I'm going to sit on the throne, all this emotion has got my guts turning flips, and then afterwards, if you want, because I think it'll be OK now, you can cut my hair."

The god of bikers exists, of that there is no doubt, a guy who rides a Heritage Classic. And he has enough of a sly sense of humour to bring together, in the same communion, the prison alpha male and his appointed deputy.

The place is calm tonight. The tension that built up during the day has dropped off. In quarters as close as ours, the atmosphere can go sour fast, with bad moods and outbursts. They are like an approaching storm. The air buzzes with positive ions that weigh upon us. But this time, our routine has come out on top and my cellmate fell asleep like a child who has gotten his favourite toy back. The prison slumbers, guards and inmates sleep, only one person keeps watch and that is me, with Winona, Nouk and the pastor by my side. I waited long enough for them to come. And now they are here. My eyes wide open. So many things to say. Their company is, and will be, all that I have left.

.   .   .

As had been decided, I was imprisoned in the Bordeaux estab-lishment, on Gouin Boulevard West, on the banks of the Rivière des Prairies, an insult's throw away from my home in the Excelsior. Destiny must have wanted to confine me to this dis-trict, for it had me meet Winona on the same boulevard, along the same river that served as a base for a number of small float-planes that offered service to the bush for those who needed it, transporting freight and passengers from lake to lake in a 300-kilometre range around Montreal. The small company Winona Mapachee worked for was called Beav'Air, a pun based on the brand of the three planes it used, all Beaver DHC-2s built by De Havilland, indestructible, little single-engine jobs that have been flying through the world's skies since August 16, 1947, the date of the maiden flight. These planes can adapt to whatever whims nature has to offer, and according to the season and the surface, they can land on floats, wheels or skis.

On that morning in May 1995, Noël Alexandre, our build-ing's prime minister, asked me if I had time to go a little fur-ther into the northern reaches of the city, to Gouin Boulevard East, not far from the Saint Joseph Park island, and pick up a friend who was coming in by floatplane around noon.

It was hardly a beauty spot, but it corresponded to the rustic bush plane standards and services that the company provided. A sheltered bay outside of the river current, a small wooden shed where the paperwork was done, and solid pon-toons to help the passengers in and out of the aircraft and tie up the planes.

With the characteristic sound of its Pratt & Whitney engine, the plane came in from the north. Slowly dropping in altitude, it flew over the landing location, heading south, then made a 180-degree turn and came in face to the water, placing its floats on the surface and sliding towards the shore like a large waterfowl in need of a break. On board were three passengers, including Alexandre's friend, Mr Nova, with three travel bags, his muddy dog and a collection of fishing rods. As I was trying to extirpate the material from the cabin, someone said to me, "You'll never make it like that." The voice belonged to Winona Mapachee, the Beaver's pilot, who grabbed the baggage and stacked it perfectly on the riverbank. I watched her check the floatplane's tie-up points, open a side compartment, take out her maps and a leather satchel, then stride off in her sea-blue pilot's outfit towards the shed that apparently served as company headquarters, stop-off point, counter, waiting room and restaurant, with its vending machine that sold granola bars and muffins packaged in cellophane.

"Everything OK? Your dog alright? Your bags are there. Everything's paid for, you can go." Elapsed time: fifteen seconds. In a relationship, it generally does not take long to understand the sort of woman you have met. In the first few seconds, I understood that Winona Mapachee, of Algonquin father and Irish mother, belonged to the category of women who live with the knowledge that life is too short and precious to waste trying to solve second-level problems.

Logic would have had our relationship ending there, a hurried exit from the rear end of a Beaver, on the banks of the Rivière des Prairies, along Gouin Boulevard. But life, and the way it likes to throw the dice, has a way of bringing people together, better to destroy them. The tool it used was

Noël Alexandre's absent-minded friend, who had me rushing back in the direction of the woman who would become my wife. It was this easy, and this simple. Nova had forgotten all his papers, his credit cards and passport in a bag inside the fishing cabin, two hours north of the city, on Sacacomie Lake, near Saint-Alexis-des-Monts. And he was in no shape to go in search of his belongings, since a sudden case of lumbago had him bedridden. A second time, Alexandre asked me if I would be so kind as to play the carrier pigeon, and fly up to Maskinongé to pick up what had to be retrieved.

Winona checked my seat belt and harness, started the engine, threw a few switches and took us gently away from the shore, then positioned the plane in the middle of the river. What came next was like nothing I had ever known. Like a Canada goose getting airborne, the Beaver pushed its floats against the surface of the water, and, as it gained speed, pulled slowly away from the current and rose into the sky, rattling with the normal racket of vibrations from a machine built in the 1950s. The weather was spring-like, and Winona flew by sight, occasionally bouncing over invisible turbulence. The entire cartography of the territory was written in her memory, and like the V-shaped flight of those same Canada geese in their great migrations, she oriented herself according to an instinct that always brought her to where she wanted to be. Suddenly, the lake appeared like an actor stepping on stage. She made her usual approach among the islands that dotted the lake, lined up the nose of the craft with some invisible landmark, and touched down with the tips of her feet, then taxied gently towards the shore. When the engine uproar died down, all I could hear was the sound of water lapping against the side of the floats.

The floating dock, the rustic shed, Nova's bag, its cavern of treasures, the sounds of the forest, the flight of the birds, the feeling of being in the right place at the right time. Winona's eyes told me the time was now, her hands slipped into my pockets, I felt the touch of her fingertips, my hands held a miracle, the friction of our clothing, the whispering of our bodies, the voice of our skin, the world down to this, the outside world with all its business, its rotten swimming pools and methods of payment, the world of the Swiss and the Danish, the world whose ventilation system I inspected every day, that world disappeared for the time the light burned inside us, this brief illumination of our lives rising upwards like a distress flare.

Winona had a very direct manner of considering and acting on things. After she put her pilot's suit back on and lit a cigarette, she told me, "When I saw you coming back to the floatplane base, the first thing I thought was, 'I'm going to spend the rest of my life with that man.' Now, let's get moving. Close the door tight and don't forget the bag."

Winona took the Beaver for a little walk on the water, sweeping past the islands like a paddler in a canoe, disturbing a small colony of otters and a few exhausted migratory birds, then she turned the nose south. She fed gas to the jets of the R-985 Wasp Junior radial engine, and the 450 horses of its nine single-row cylinders transmitted their power to the double-bladed Hamilton Standard propeller, which proceeded to patiently cut through the air resistance to take us back to Montreal, bag in hand, hearts on our sleeves.

For the eleven years of our non-standard marriage, I never stopped loving Winona Mapachee, not even for the blink of an eye. Ever since that day at the lake, she has been a part of my flesh, I bear her within me, she lives, thinks, moves in my heart, and her death has changed nothing of that.

A few weeks later, I went to see Noël Alexandre to tell him how he had changed the course of my life on two occasions. First by entrusting me with the captaincy of this great ocean liner of a building, and then by sending me on a honeymoon by plane to Sacacomie Lake. "You're married, Paul?" I was. Of course, it all depended what you thought about non-standard unions. Administratively, Her Majesty in London and her Parisian counterpart would no doubt consider us as ordinary *concubini*, a Latin noun that can be translated as "bed partners". That was neither an insult, nor totally false. But were we to stand in the gaze of the Grand Chief of the Algonquins, Tessouat of the Kichesipirini nation, there was no doubt that, even though he had been dead since 1636, this sage would have declared Winona and me man and wife. That is exactly what my concubine explained to me when, after some time of living together, I asked her if she wanted us to get married. "But we already are. Among the Algonquin, there's no contract or promises to pronounce. Two people live with one another and for one another. When they are no longer happy together, they separate." And that was how, with an extreme economy of language and in four sentences, the Queen of England and her common law were shipped back to their damp island.

In my eyes, Winona represented the wonderful essence of two ancient worlds. From her Irish mother, she inherited the strength to take on the earth with all life had given her, pushing aside obstacles, making each day with her own two hands. Playful, good-natured, unfailingly loyal, she had a hereditary distrust of the British. From her Algonquin side, she received the ability to flow into the world of intangible things and be one with it, reading messages sent by the wind, the curtains of rain, the creaking branches of the trees. She grew up in the halls of legends, the enlightening stories that rework the origins of time, that tell how wolves taught men to speak, taught them about love, mutual respect and the art of living in groups. And bears, too. And caribou. They were our ancestors, as were eagles, the trees of the forest, the grass of the prairies. We all ate of the same earth, and, when the time came, it would eat us, too.

But really, outside of a few centres of her brain that were deeply Algonquin, Winona was a pragmatic woman who lived inside the body of airplanes. She knew that every day, their wings and their bellies had to be checked for signs of wear.

Every morning, when I look at the photo of my wife, I still do not know if I loved an Irishwoman from Galway or a beauty from Maniwaki. Like the sublime light of Skagen, her features changed as the hours passed, and one branch of her origins would take precedence over the other. When she awoke, her copper hair and pale eyes opened onto the antechamber of the Gaels. But as evening crept near, the low rays of the sun showed the imprint of the Native nations on her skin colour, the bones of her face and the steadiness of her gaze. I found such pleasure in that ambivalence, and lived secretly with two women at once, finding consolation with one when the other left me out in the cold. No, I never stopped loving Winona Mapachee for a second.

My routine in the building was shaken up for a while when she decided to come and live in my little apartment. We did not have much room, but the proximity served only to bring us closer. To trundle off early in the morning to examine the Excelsior's respiratory system became much less interesting and returning late after my last duties as chief cook and bottle washer seemed like a waste of time. It is not easy taking care of a building and a woman at the same time, coddling a couple dozen widows while trying to charm your wife. Winona's schedule changed according to the seasons, just as, in Montreal, the places she could land changed depending on whether she was using floats, wheels or, in winter, skis. Our life as a couple had long days that sometimes went much later than we would have preferred. But as Kieran Read had taught me, such good advice, I did everything possible so that on the day of my funeral, Winona could, in front of the witnesses gathered there, assure our insurance broker that, within our "loyal family sexuality", she had known only "satisfying and frequent relations".

During the first years of our marriage, things began to change at the Excelsior. The population was ageing. The retirees were moving into the final chapter of their lives. They began losing all sorts of little things, forgetting their keys and belongings by the pool, worrying about unimportant details, calling me in the evening to report strange noises in their ventilation ducts. They were getting old. Not all of them were dying, but all were weakened.

The Excelsior was slowly entering a dark age. In 1977, just before Christmas, I saw Soraya Engelbrecht, an aged resident from the fifth floor, walk into the lobby at ten in the evening in her nightgown and sit down in an armchair there. Outside, the cold froze the snowflakes in their flight. I was finishing putting up the decorations, a longstanding tradition that the owners insisted on. I put aside my work and went to check on the old lady. She gazed at me with benevolent kindness, but I realised she did not recognise me. I slipped my jacket over her shoulders. "It's me, Paul. I'll help you back to your apartment. You can't stay here, you'll catch cold. Come, I'll walk you back, we'll go together." Her apartment door was locked. I let myself in with my passkey. Mrs Engelbrecht looked at me as if I were a magician, and suddenly she knew who I was. She thanked me and begged my pardon. "I'm sorry, Paul. I'm sorry for all this. I've been very tired lately." She walked to her bed, lay down, and closed her eyes immediately. I pulled a blanket over her, turned off the light, and kept watch for a moment in the darkness.

Soraya Engelbrecht had always said she had no family, and I did not know who to contact for help. A week later, again at nightfall, as I waited for Winona, looking out the lobby window, I spotted the old lady crossing the street, barefoot and without a coat, then going to sit on the bench by the bus stop. It must have been minus ten and the pavement was icy. When she caught sight of me, she tried to get to her feet, then held out her hand. "It's horrible, Paul, I believe William has died. I think my husband just .died." I gathered up Soraya Engelbrecht in my arms and carried her into the building. She

159

weighed no more than a child. I took her to her apartment and stayed until she fell into sleep. She had lost her husband a dozen years earlier. His name was Frederic Edward.

This difficult episode was the first of many. As the years passed, my new role as social worker began to take over from my maintenance duties. I alerted Noël Alexandre about Mrs Engelbrecht's condition, and he contacted the local community health centre, which helped place Soraya in an appropriate long-term care facility, with her consent. I prepared a small bag so she would have everything she needed in her new residence. On her way out, she made me promise to water her plants. When the medical team came to pick her up, I walked her to the vehicle. Then I went upstairs and closed down the apartment, shutting the door on everything her life had been.

Fortunately, that evening I was back with Winona. Safely home after her day's flights, overflowing with negative ions, the kind that cleanse the soul, refreshed by the beauty she had seen, those timeless landscapes a hundred miles from old age and hospices, a thousand miles from my little world of six declining floors. In her ancestors' language, Winona means "first-born daughter". More than ever, for me, Winona was my one and only.

I remember the end of the 1990s as a time of exodus, with the departure of numerous owners, more than a dozen at least, who did not have the physical strength or the emotional resources to live with their solitude, despite the care lavished on the lawns, flowerbeds, the perfect temperature and texture of the pool, the efficiency of the machinery and the constant availability of the superintendent. Often I ran errands for the owners, and made trips to the pharmacy, keeping watch over my little club of widows, who hung on to life by the tips of their polished fingernails. I knew it would all break down sooner or later, but when their sink leaked or their kitchen air filter needed replacing, I ran to their side and did the job, and reassured them that I was still there. After all this time spent in the great house, I came to understand that these people meant something to me, and, in my way, I loved them.

Before the Shadows Fall

SINCE HIS MEETING with the warden, Patrick Horton is a changed man, more concerned with the world around him and, this morning at least, with the way the banks have conspired to destroy our future. "Fuck, did you see that? The subprime mess is worse than ever. They made their first estimates of how much that bullshit has cost us. Do you know how much retired people in the States have gotten ripped off for, with their pensions and all? Go ahead, name me a figure. Come on, don't be afraid, give me an amount. You're nowhere near it, man. Two thousand billion dollars. I don't know how many zeros you'd have to put after the two. Two thousand billion dollars, and that's just in the States alone. Can you imagine for the rest of the world? No shit! You kick someone's ass who needs kicking, and they put you inside for two years. Meanwhile, they're cleaning out the casino and stealing from orphans and widows, and afterwards, they go sun themselves in Acapulco and snort lines through hundred-dollar bills. My mother had some bucks in that outfit, not piles and piles, but for her it must have meant something. The guy from the bank told her it all went down the drain. Everybody got ripped off and he spends all day telling them the same thing. Down the drain. Did you have anything invested in that tub?"

Nothing, Patrick. I never put down a single dollar betting. Winona and I lived one day at a time. Our money did not do the work, we did. And what we did not spend slept quietly at the Bank of Montreal on Saint-Jacques Street.

"Could you calculate how many Harleys two thousand billion would get you if I gave you the exact price of a Fat Boy?" Despite his brand-new interest in the world that he has suddenly decided to join, with Patrick there always comes a time when fiction catches up to reality and starts manhandling it. "When it comes to calculating the operation and all that, I think I could figure it out, but with all the zeros, I know I'm going to screw up." For Patrick, the world with its crises and misfortunes can be understood and interpreted using the baseline of the sole stable value of reference on this earth: the Harley Fat Boy.

"You know, when I read stuff like that, stories about the banks and the whole shitstorm around them, I tell myself there are so many things I don't understand about economics and politics, too many, there's no hope of me catching up, I'm way too far behind. Then other times it's the opposite, I try and hang on, and remind myself that the more things I know, the less chance I'll get reamed out, when it comes to voting or investing my money. On the other hand, right now there's no problem because I don't have a cent."

· · ·

In late summer of 1999, I was called to the deck of the Excelsior pool. Noël Alexandre had suffered an attack of some kind. He was lying on the ground. His eyes seemed to be searching for a face, something to fasten on to. I took his hand in mine and told him all the useless things that come to mind when misfortune intrudes onto our daily tasks, just as we are looking for the attachment for the ratchet wrench.

I rode with him in the ambulance, and never let go of the hand he had so often offered me.

I returned to the building at nightfall. The pool was deserted, and the door to the machine shed was still open. The part was still waiting to be attached to the ratchet wrench.

Winona had returned home. On the sofa, lying at her feet, a little dog with white fur was curled up in a ball, sleeping. A female, she told me. "I found her this afternoon. She was abandoned by Lake Manitou, over near Sainte-Agathe-des-Monts. She was starving, and had an abscess in one paw. She can't be more than six or seven months old. We'll keep her. She's like a baby wolf." Nouk was neither a she-wolf nor a show dog, but a wondrous animal, subtle, curious about discovering and learning the world, attentive to our pain even before we felt it. The dog quickly became an indissociable part of our lives, and she fit in with incredible ease, jumping into the Beaver when it came time to deliver a fisherman to his fish, or running alongside me through Ahuntsic Park. After a fall of fluffy snow, she would roll in it until her fur was saturated, engorged with winter's gift that weighed her down, then shake herself off, sending a second snowstorm into the icy air.

Nouk ate with us, watched movies with us and slept next to us, once she had turned around four or five times, as her ancestors had taught her to, according to the rules of her species and the laws of the forest.

In the evening, as we awaited Winona's return, Nouk would come and slip her nose between my arm and my floating ribs. And in this shadowy hideout where nothing could happen and that she alone knew, she would help me understand all kinds of things that men often have trouble saying out loud. Sometimes she would half-open one eye, just to let me know that she was going to be quiet and have a short nap. There was so much awareness and loyalty in that little animal that, as time went by, I began to speak to her the way I would to another person, sharing the rhythm and burdens of my days with her. None of that was incongruous – that was the most surprising thing. I would babble away from where I sat and Nouk listened and understood me in her way. She agreed to make the effort to decode the encryptions of man, and I did the same and deciphered her varieties of barking and read her body language. Just like with anything else, after my apprenticeship, I reached a fairly satisfying result that let us both deal with the essential matters of daily life, since we now spoke the same language. She read me like an open book, I was attentive to her, and generous with my tenderness, as we naturally are when we love someone.

Noël Alexandre came back to the Excelsior some ten days after he was hospitalised. What the health system sent back to us was a fragile envelope into which a little life had been breathed. His emaciated face covered in age spots showed his cheekbones, the hinge of his jaws, the deep-set caverns of his eyes. The skin of his temples was transparent, and beneath the hanging drapery of his neck, the weak efforts of his heart were written.

Noël Alexandre had been sent back to the Excelsior to die.

I set up his hospital-style bed and IV in front of the bay window. The uppermost branches of the maples seemed to be seeking entry there. Nurses came by three times a day to give him the care he needed, and day and night I was connected to him by an invisible thread that owed as much to the miracles of electronics as it did those of affection. He simply had to press the little alarm button he kept in the palm of his hand and I would drop all my maintenance work.

The alarm rang often, and each time I managed to cobble together the illusion that he was doing better.

And then, one day, the alarm stopped ringing.

All those years, the President, as I called him, was able to give a soul and a spirit to the building, and slowly it took on his image, offering its residents a climate of well-being, protective yet open. By the force of his attitude, and his courage when it was necessary, Noël Alexandre accomplished quite the feat. He tuned the hormones of sixty-seven other owners, often motivated by conflicting desires and feelings, and he convinced them to show respect and tolerance towards the others. Using his *savoir faire* and dispensing sage recipes, he led our great house with intelligence until his mandate was finished.

Just before the end of the millennium, a few months before the rest of the world, we entered a new era about which we knew nothing. But something was floating in the air, and it led us to believe that, in many ways, the new era would be less noble, less gentle and less rich than the preceding one.

At the very end of the year, on December 30, the general assembly brought the owners together. The reports were read out, followed by the election of the new administrator. Even Kieran Read attended and participated in the vote. There were three candidates for Noël's job. Louis Angelin, a representative of the old school, the little duke of the third floor who kept a sharp eye on the swimming pool costs. He was intransigent when it came to lawn maintenance, being a botanist manqué, and was as boring as a rainy day. Edouard Sedgwick, made in New England, a new arrival from the new school, with a new car, new wife and apparently a new life, a former resident of the chic Outremont district, recently demoted to the fifth floor of an Ahuntsic condo. His first request the day he moved in: the notes from the last co-owners' meeting. And then there was Madeleine Brigg, the envied shareholder of the top floor, a reconditioned sixty-year-old with a devastating sense of humour, but delicious, unpredictable and a woman of some accomplishment who was in charge of the collections at the MAC, the city's Musée d'art contemporain. Our building was too dreary in her opinion. A few Tinguely sculptures set up in the garden would remedy that. Out of touch with reality, absolutely incapable of managing a building like the Excelsior, but, all the same, a wonderful person to spend time with on a daily basis.

Each candidate was allocated fifteen minutes to describe the way they saw the building's future. No surprise: Angelin expounded on seeds and lawn fertiliser, the vegetalisation of the ground-floor common areas, with a detour regarding the costs of heating and maintaining the pool. Brigg offered a short class in the art history of "machines, movement and sound", and shared her enthusiasm for a more stimulating environment, with a garden – again, no surprise – dotted with inventions by Tinguely (1925–1991). Or, failing that, since we would never have the adequate means, the works of young Canadian sculptors the building could acquire, whose costs could eventually be written off. Someone objected: "But we don't pay taxes, we're not looking for deductions." Brigg dismissed the argument with an imperious nod of her chin, then sat down.

Even before he opened his mouth, and a single word was spoken, I knew he would be elected. The perfect profile of the overdressed fop. The archetypal sly swindler, the sneaky jackal. With his know-how concerning our modern times, a mix of familiarity and arrogance and contempt, Edouard Sedgwick was our man, a fervent toad that Nouk and I sniffed out from a hundred paces, presenting himself as the "guarantor of everyone's welfare, promising to keep a scrupulous eye on all categories of expenses so that every dollar spent is put to good use, so that this building, with its remodelled management, will remain the home for all of us". Amen.

Angelin's verdant campaign garnered him fourteen votes, essentially from the great plains of the old-timers, no doubt attached to the nostalgia of their greener years. Brigg picked up seven votes, including mine and Kieran Read's and five other electors who figured that, since they were going to disappear, they might as well go out with a bang. And Sedgwick, with his miserable clichés, his bean-counter's logic, sucked up all the rest, except for one abstention, forty-six votes spirited away. It was both consternating and magical to watch the con artist at work, equipped with a rabbit and the hat that goes with it. Forty-six votes that cast forty-six handfuls of dirt on Noël Alexandre's tomb. Forty-six votes captured by a man who came out of nowhere, whom no-one had known a month earlier. Forty-six votes that were going to make my life increasingly unpleasant. Forty-six votes from people I had helped and supported in the past.

A plebiscite for the new age.

The millennium that was beginning and the world that would go with it belonged to Edouard Sedgwick.

Happily, Winona and Nouk could sometimes lift me out of this universe where I had been a prisoner for far too long. The Beaver would take us for weekends to a camp on the banks of Lac Saint-Jean. I loved those flights in the racket of the old craft shaken by its engine's fits and starts. I made a small flexible cap to protect Nouk's ears from the decibels. At first she hated the accessory, but soon grew accustomed to it. We could have lingered in the skies for ever, and taken the time to see everything from above, the trees and water, the land and its animals. We soared above a world without end that opened up the big book of its beauty for all infinity. Vastness was all, the sky, the water, the forests full of invisible wildlife, one day we had deserted all that and set up shop in six-storey buildings with intercoms and a small artificial lake from which no-one drank. We lived and walked along these artificial waters without leaving the slightest trace, except for the keyboards of our code pads.

What I saw from the plane belonged to no-one, no one man, and not even two for that matter. What would a country have done with all this space? Here was a world without royalty and trusts, where a crown of forty-six votes meant nothing, was worth nothing, preserved nothing. With forty-six votes, you could not eat or save yourself. With forty-six votes, you baited bears, set wolf traps or starved to death.

The noise in the Beaver was so deafening that ear protection was of almost no use, and Winona and I learned how to communicate in sign language. When she pointed her fingers downwards, I understood we were going to descend and land soon. That was the only part of our trips that I feared. The instant when the floats touched water. Despite their design, and the aerodynamic explanations my wife supplied, I was always afraid that one of the appendages, the way a sailboat might do, would enter the water too deeply and, propelled by our speed, throw itself over head first, launching our craft into a somersault. Which is why, before touching down on the surface of a lake, I always set Nouk on my lap and held her tightly until the plane confirmed our survival and guaranteed we were safe.

In a magazine that specialised in this kind of thing, I read a disturbing article about an exhaustive study that, while praising the Beaver's solid performance and versatility, also warned pilots about a tendency the plane had. "At low speeds, inclined and heavily loaded, the Beaver has a reputation for being unpredictable, and no advance signs prepare the pilot for a stall.

The shock is sudden, and at low altitude, it is often very difficult to right the craft, which may lead to a fatal outcome."

When I showed Winona the piece, she told me, "I know all
about that. Everyone has known about it since 1946. But those
guys wrote one article about the Beaver, and I fly it every day.
Anyway, I always have the hummingbird with me."

The hummingbird was a keychain that never left her side.
The little metal bird, she believed, was her guardian angel that
had the power to keep a Beaver on the straight and narrow.
My wife was totally fascinated by the bird, a myth in South
America, the harbinger of a thousand contradictory outcomes,
the vector of happiness and prosperity among the Taíno,
though in Brazil, it telegraphed your death if it got into your
house.

This tiny bird is one of nature's riddles, a minuscule mon-
ster of a machine designed by an engineer with a degree in
aerodynamics and a vicious sense of humour who teamed up
with a trickster anatomist. The animal, five or six centimetres
in length, features a heart that beats 1,260 times a minute and
lungs that breathe 500 times during the same period. Its wings
can pivot in any direction, allowing it to fly just as fast backwards as forwards, or up and down, and hit 100 kilometres
an hour while maintaining a variety of unlikely positions. Its
wings beat 200 times a second and whip up bubbles of air,
creating vortexes on demand. It is also the world's specialist
when it comes to static flight and quick changes in direction,
and boasts of 6,590,000 red blood cells per cubic millimetre.
It can transport its few grams of mass over a distance of
800 kilometres, requiring nourishment eight times an hour

except during periods of migration. Before surrendering to sleep, it lowers its body temperature ten degrees by reducing its frenetic heart rate to fifty beats a minute. Such is the unlikely animal to which my wife entrusted her life and fate. A three-gram bird responsible for saving a stalled-out Beaver weighing two and a half tons. Every time I saw Winona's keychain, I thought of my father. If he had heard my wife confess her belief, he would have surely concluded that her act of faith, tested every day in the uproar of the skies, was a much-needed lesson for a pastor and his binoculars.

Since his visit with the warden, Patrick has wanted only one thing – to go back there. A few days ago, he sent an application to the chief guard to be given that privilege, but his request got nowhere. He was not so easily discouraged; he sat down at his table and wrote Savage a letter. He scribbled his way across a number of sheets of paper before judging the results satisfactory. Then he slipped his mystery missive into an envelope and gave it to a guard to give to its addressee. Four days later, he had his answer. A large file that contained exactly what he wished for. "Shit, Savage is the real thing. No kidding, he's great. Can you imagine, I send him a letter asking him if he can get me the latest Harley parts and accessories catalogue. And that's exactly what he sends me: this year's catalogue. Which means when the guy knocked off work, he went straight and got it for me. The guy's a good Samaritan, there's no other way to put it. I'm going to write him a thank-you note." He sat down at his table again and began the letter. It kept him busy for at least an hour. "When I start, do I say 'Dear Manu' or 'Dear Mr Savage'? But who cares, among bikers, there aren't jailbirds and screws, we're all the same, we all have the same motto engraved on the engine housing, 'Live to Ride, Ride to Live'. Manu sounds cooler, more Harley. 'Dear Mr' is too stiff, it's like a guy sending you an electric bill. After all, we had a good talk. If you'd seen the look on his face when he started telling me about his Heritage, you'd understand he's more of a 'Manu' than a 'Mr'. So, help me, man, Manu or Mr?"

In the end, I convinced him that although the second term of address partook less of the biker world of cubic inches, it had the advantage of being more conventional. By making sure he would not get on the warden's bad side by being over-familiar, he left the door open to making another request. My last argument tipped the scales. "Shit, man, you're making sense, you're like one of those chess guys that can figure things out nineteen moves ahead of time. You're right. Dear Mr Savage, that's the way to go." Patrick did not ask me to vet the contents of the message, and I was afraid the biker in him would pop out, and that some formula that was a little too friendly, like "Fuck, man", would intrude and ruin his efforts to stay on the praiseworthy straight and narrow.

Once the thank-you note was safely sent off, Patrick paged through the catalogue, line by line, truly savouring it, sipping each section like fine wine. I could picture him installing, mentally at least, all the accessories one by one on his Fat Boy, stepping back to admire the effect, then taking off whatever gadget it was and trying out something new, an aesthetic and mechanical variation, leather saddlebags or a new exhaust system, mini-ape handlebars or lounge-style footrests. At times like that, he was in his mental safe, locked and double dead-bolted, inaccessible and happy the way he rarely was, infinitely on his own, without a father or memories or police record, a virgin past and an empty present, born to live and ride, or, more like it, ride and live.

I do not have this kind of mental meadow to set my mind free and let it ramble. I am completely a prisoner. Locked in. This place owns me and flays me a little deeper each day. True, I have my visits. But some days, the dead are like the rest of us, they have trouble living. Nouk did not come today, and neither did my father. But Winona dropped in. She was not carrying the house keys or the metal hummingbird. She did not feel much like talking. This time her face was so Irish it faded into the mists of Galway Bay and the smell of the Corrib River. I remember once in Toulouse, I do not recall exactly what the occasion was, my father gave a sermon based on Irish peat moss, comparing that organic fossil matter to some other substance that stratified our lives. Often it was not easy to follow my father through the maze of his mystical comparisons.

In four hours, darkness will fall. I hope sleep will not refuse me. It is the small opening in my brain I can slip into and escape for a few hours. When I cannot do that, when I can't find the way out, I take a little lorazepam that, with a lactose-based excipient, will handle the problem.

From time to time, I hear the sound of a page turning. Then I know Patrick is happy.

· · ·

Winona moving in with me did not really change Kieran Read's habits. When he felt the need to confide, he would come and visit me a little earlier, and we would examine our worlds together. He was deeply disappointed by Sedgwick's election, and believed he could not be trusted. "He talks like a financial planning brochure, and I know he's going to turn this building upside down. I know that kind of guy, I deal with them every day. Cost killers, they're called. They have an Excel spreadsheet in their heads, and they're ruining our society. Keep your eyes open, Paul. You're the superintendent, and you're managing the budget, which means you're on the front line. He'll be looking over your shoulder and counting everything twice, checking every penny."

When Winona came in, Nouk showed her unbridled joy, and Kieran, with his casualty adjuster mug, pretended to head for the door. His performance was so weak Winona asked him to stay for dinner. His face lit up with happiness and gratitude like a man who has been saved *in extremis* from an evening alone with himself.

My wife was fascinated by the specimens of humanity he set on the table before us as he shared the catalogue of his observations. "The job I do has one enormous advantage. It opens the door onto the smelly barnyard of our world, the places where a man's price is totalled up and his value nego-tiated, where everything is costed out and paid for, where people end up in court for reasons no-one should ever know about, and for stories you can't believe ever happened. Back in the day, I worked on the Ford Pinto story, I don't know if you remember that. In the 1970s, Ford built this subcompact that wasn't much to look at. The company quickly realised there was a major construction problem. The metal used for the gas tank was extremely thin, so the cars were quick to catch on fire if they were hit from behind. There were one hundred and eighty deaths, people burned alive in their cars, another one hundred and eighty badly burnt victims, and seven thousand automobiles turned to ash. There was obviously a structural problem, so the company's top brass commissioned an in-house study to evaluate the cost of carrying out the necessary modifications. The analysts came back with a report that came to be known as the 'Pinto Memo: Cost–Benefit Analysis'. The conclusion? To indemnify the victims' families would be much cheaper than the amount of money the company would have to set aside to recall all Pinto models and replace the faulty gas tanks. Ford put the report on a dark shelf somewhere, and its customers continued going up in smoke inside their Pintos. Until, one day, the scandal forced the firm to reveal how the calculations had been made, and the inhumane choices that were involved. Ford took out its chequebook and settled the issue by allotting $200,000 to each victim, $67,000 to those who suffered burns, and $700 per destroyed vehicle.

"The Pinto affair is only the tip of the iceberg, the part of the world you can see where the worth of human beings is negotiated, above an infraworld where the lives of human beings, real as they once were, are calculated on the basis of ratios that are no more than the work of accountants. I remember a few years ago, a bill concerning these issues was introduced in the US Senate. Among other things, it stated that using dollars to determine the value of a life, when a decision had to be made, was profoundly offensive to the religions, ethnic beliefs, and shared morals of the people of the nation. The bill also mentioned that the use of racial criteria and factors that took into account income, state of health, age and disability should also be banned. After the insurance company lobby got its claws into it, the bill was rejected, then thrown into the shredder. Now, Paul, you might say there's no comparison, and that I'm exaggerating, but a guy like Sedgwick, and I know of what I speak, could very well have written the Pinto Memo."

Nouk came and nestled her nose in the crook of my elbow to tell me, once again, in her words, the story of the day when a strange motorised bird landed on the water of her lake, and an Algonquin woman with Irish tendencies stepped out, walked towards her, offered her hand, gave her some cookies and sat down next to her, even as she was trembling with fear, fatigue and fever. The woman examined her wound, petted her for a while, picked her up in her arms and placed her in the airplane.

At that point in the story, Nouk lifted her nose out of its warm, protective shelter and looked up at me. I swore I heard her say, "Then I was so tired I fell asleep, even with all the racket the plane was making."

Kieran paid tribute to Winona's cooking and thanked her for a "real family evening". I understood what the adjuster meant, but the sudden expansion of our household and the celebration of our new bond seemed a little premature.

In a building, or in a community, misfortune generally settles in for a while. For months, it will stalk the hallways, going from door to door, picking off the weakest, ruining the hopeful. Then, one day, it will change streets, or neighbour-hoods, carrying out its blind craft. In our case, that "while" lasted nearly a year. All manner of plagues fell upon the Excelsior, its machines, its trees and its people.

It started with the great ice storm that paralysed the city for a good ten days. Under the weight of the accumulated ice, everything started falling: pylons, power lines, phone lines, transformers blew in a domino effect, and the region was cast into darkness. Without heat, the apartments turned into freezers. The first day, the residents tried to stay warm in their bathrooms by huddling next to their tubs, which contained what remained of the hot water. The building had two energy supplies. Electricity for operating the thermostats, and gas to heat the hot water that ran through the radiators. Wearing jackets and shrouded in blankets like indigents, the owners wandered through the halls and common areas in search of the latest news and whatever comfort it might bring. Without lifts, the oldest ones stayed in their units, and I found a way to bring them food and water. The hardiest tried to go to work, defying an icy world hung with stalactites that dripped from the trees. Everywhere, a sense of the unreal. When evening fell, the night was unbroken blackness on all sides. As if life had turned off the switch. At times we would hear a branch crack and fall with a crash of splintering ice. Unable to throw off its heavy overcoat, the big yellow birch in the garden began to bend, then it split in two as if sliced down the middle by an axe fallen from heaven. After a difficult week, little by little the lights began reappearing in the district. Halos of hope glowed here and there through the ice. Meanwhile, the Excelsior remained in darkness. I spent my days running errands to the market to supply my widows and older residents. I did it by foot on sidewalks and streets shining like skating rinks. The bags, the stairs, go up, go down, explain that I can't do anything about the weather, chip away the ice from around the front door, throw sand in front of the garage and the walkways to the building, disarm the electronics and electrical system, thaw out whatever can be thawed, take the chainsaw to the birch tree branches. Look after Winona, whose plane has been grounded, and find a way to warm up Nouk, who seems to be asking herself what is going on in the white man's world.

In the Ahuntsic district, we were one of the last buildings to be reconnected. One morning, the lift doors opened and closed, the water in the bathtubs went down the drain, the extractors went back to extracting. Conduit after conduit, power flowed into the plugs, and life settled back into a cocoon of twenty-one degrees, the ideal temperature for the comfort of the species as decreed by the assembly of owners.

The ice storm caused damage and distress, and it also weakened people. In less than a week, ambulances stopped in front of our lobby to take two widows to the hospital, each with a case of double pneumonia. A sexagenarian from the third floor was evacuated with a suspected heart attack. And then Mr Sibelius – a wonderful old man of an age beyond numbers, the product of a distant era who swam for his life and complimented me every time he saw me on the "texture" of the water in the pool – broke his hip when he fell on the ribbon of ice on the sidewalk across the street. During this period, which was an ordeal for me as well, nowhere did I see in any part of our great house the figure, not even a fleeting trace, of our new administrator, who never once enquired after our state, or the condition of the property.

At the end of the winter, after a lingering illness staved off by bottled oxygen, Edmonde Clarence, one of our widows, fell victim to a pneumococcus as a nurse was coming to check the proper functioning of her equipment. Madame Clarence's daughter arrived at the Excelsior a few minutes later, but the hardest work had already been done.

The events began to gnaw away at me. I watched our little community falling apart, and my position at its very centre meant I would have to endure the worst of them. Sometimes, on certain evenings, I would need to knock on Kieran Read's door to confide in him some of what I was seeing, and what I was thinking.

I tried to keep Winona separate from this little world that meant nothing to her, just a club of co-owners who, if you thought about it, would not have lasted long in her forests.

So many winters spent here, between these walls. And as many autumns and summers.

Time was passing, and all I saw of the world was the view from the summit of the roof or the depths of the pool. The years were ticking off, and my job as a model servant was beginning to unravel.

The beginning of July was marked by a series of technical problems that seemed to have conspired to make all the Excelsior's mechanical systems go haywire at once. It began with the lifts. The doors opened and closed, but the car refused to move. The motherboard that ran the movement functions had broken down. As an apparent consequence of the ice invasion during the storm, half of the extractor motors overheated and burned out. I spent days on the roof repairing them, melting in the open-air furnace. Shortly afterwards, the entire electronic system that governed access to the building failed. At the end of a nightmarish day, as I was coming in through the door, the phone rang. "What's going on, Paul? Nothing works anymore. People are calling up and complaining. What are you doing, are you in charge or not? You have to get on top of things, and fast. I heard you were changing the extractors. That's going to cost us a fortune. I want to see the bills on the weekend. Did the electronic entry guys come? No, Paul, no, you have to get on them, show some guts, I'm not going to do it for you." Sedgwick. In all his glory. Sedgwick jerking his superintendent's chain, getting him back in line, where he belonged, reminding him who was running the show.

The worst event of that dark year occurred on the first week of August. To repair the fifth-floor facade damaged by the ice, I hired a company that specialised in that kind of task. Three brick-workers arrived to tuckpoint the sections that the ice had undone. A week's work. Scaffolding was set up and the weather was favourable for the upcoming period, except for the risk of an occasional shower.

On that day, before noon, I was cutting the grass by the main entrance. Through the roar of the machine and the ear protection I was wearing, I heard a scream.

He was lying on the ground in an impossible position, incompatible with anything a human skeleton can do. He was trying to breathe, but it was hard going. I did not dare restore that broken body to its proper shape. I took his hand, an act I had repeated many times during the year. Above, his companions shouted that he had fallen. As they cried out, they leaned over the safety bars of the scaffolding, some fifteen metres up. I had met the man who had fallen. We spoke briefly when he arrived. I remember he said he lived in Laval and every day he spent an hour on the Laurentian Expressway to get down to work. The kind of conversation you have at the beginning of a job.

I called for help and held on to his hand, comforting him with useless words. How many times had I attended to sick and dying people lately? Later, Sedgwick took it upon himself to remind me that this was not part of a superintendent's functions. From above, the petrified brick-workers stared at the scene. The man on the ground gasped for breath, but he could get no more than wisps of air. His face took on a strange colour, and his hand, still in mine, quivered with convulsions. Despite his ruined body where nothing was in the right place, he made an effort to lift his head. He opened his eyes wide, and spoke the last sentence of his life. "My dog is home all by himself." Then it was over. His neck fell back to the ground, and the way he lay there, he seemed to be watching his friends above.

Their task was absurd, but the ambulance attendants massaged his heart, and used their defibrillator and oxygen supply. They did what they were trained to do, the work carried out in the darkness that precedes the night, with hopes of bringing back the dead.

I passed on the man's final message to the crew who took

away his body. I made sure they understood. His dog was at home, all by himself. Someone had to be told. The zipper closed on the body bag; that evening, the man in a thousand pieces would not have to face the lines of snail's-pace traffic on the Laurentian Expressway.

At nine o'clock that evening, Sedgwick knocked on my door with a bailiff's heavy hand. He did not ask how the man had fallen, or whether he had suffered, or if someone should be informed. He was holding the building's insurance policy, and wanted additional information about our liability exposure when it came to work accidents involving outside contractors. When he obtained such information, he relaxed a little. "If I understand correctly, Paul, there's no problem, we're in the clear. Good. We have nothing to do with it. The dead man worked for a company, and their insurance will settle it. In the meantime, you and I are going to have to review the accident. And always check the working conditions and the liability of the companies we hire. Why did you choose them? How often have they worked for us? Three times in ten years. Well, you can scratch them off our list. By the way, is the job finished? No, no, call them and tell them to complete it according to the schedule they promised to respect. One of their workers died, that's sad, sure, but they need to find a solution and replace him."

Sedgwick. An incorruptible Gauleiter. A bastard to the core.

After that episode, the man became so odious in my sight that I could not bear to look at him. Kieran Read and a dozen other owners pooled together to buy flowers, and they asked me to take them to the brick-worker's funeral. Kieran accompanied me and we stood with a handful of strangers and the dead man's dog in front of a grave site in a Laval cemetery. The man's name was engraved on the stone. Jerome Aldegheri.

Two days later, Sedgwick summoned me to his apartment. He was outraged that I had attended the man's funeral. Like a furious medieval landowner, he berated his doltish peasant. "Things have to be clear, Paul, once and for all. I am not paying you to go to funerals or spend half your time playing social worker in the building. Let me remind you that your work stops at the door to each unit. It is up to the owners to solve their health problems, and whatever needs they have. There are associations and organisations for people in that situation. Your job is building maintenance, not maintaining the people who live here. Take no personal initiatives without clearing them with me first. And that includes taking flowers to the funeral of a man who worked here less than a week. You have equipment, a garden, common spaces, a garage and a swimming pool to keep you busy, isn't that enough? And on the subject of the pool, a point of order. As specified in your contract, neither you nor your wife are allowed to use it. Thank you for informing Madame Hansen of that fact. And your dog must be on a leash when inside the building. As well, the garden is off-limits to it. From now on, you are to be the superintendent, no more, and I am paying you quite enough for that job. Every week, you will provide an account of your expenditures, which will help us understand which costs we can reduce or eliminate altogether. I want this building to be operational twenty-four hours a day. The residents, whatever their state happens to be, must not distract you from your functions. I was elected to see to the good governance of the Excelsior, and believe me, from now on I'll be keeping an eye on your schedule and every dollar you spend."

The encounter left me humiliated and broken. The few rough-edged retorts I came up with did nothing to restore the threads of my dignity. That evening, I described the event to Winona and Kieran and announced my intention to quit. They tempered my bad mood, changed the subject, ate a slice of pizza, then my wife and I went out with the dog to walk in the warmth of the summer night.

The very next day, chance or destiny or bad luck, call it what you will, unbending and in peremptory fashion, returned to remind us that it was still living in the building and was the master of our days. And that whatever Sedgwick went on about, we would still have to deal with it.

Mr Seligman lived on the third floor with his wife. He had retired from Hydro-Québec. He enjoyed all sorts of things – bagels, smoked meat, chopped liver, hockey, Jewish jokes and especially his Lexus 4×4. Twice a week, on Mondays and Fridays, he would go down to the garage, drive his vehicle to the washing station, pull the protective curtain and embark on an hour's worth of cleaning and cosmetic treatments. He vacuumed his mats, waxed the leather seats and shined everything that wanted to sparkle. On a more prosaic note, I was working on a hot-water pipe not far from the space dedicated to automobile cleanliness.

When he saw me perched on my stepladder, Mr Seligman stopped his work and came to greet me and chew the fat, as he would say. Before turning back to the task at hand, he felt moved to tell me one of the stories that he always had on hand.

"A guy is playing golf with three rabbis who are absolutely burning up the course, while he's lagging far behind. So he asks them what their secret is. They tell him, 'It's very simple. Every day we go to the synagogue and pray with all our hearts.' So the guy runs off to the nearest synagogue and starts praying as hard as he can. He goes every day, speaks to the Lord with great devotion for a whole year, asks Him to improve his game, but he is no better a golfer than before. So he goes to see the three rabbis, who are still destroying par, and explains that, despite his prayers and all his fervour, his game is still terrible. The rabbis huddle together, then one of them says to him, 'If you don't mind me asking, what synagogue are you going to?' The guy tells him, 'You know, the big one in Outremont.' The rabbi smiles. 'No wonder you're not getting any better. That one's for tennis.'"

Proud of his small success, laughing away richly at his own joke, Thomas Seligman, a man cut from a block of good humour and optimism, told me slyly, "There will be another joke tomorrow, Paul, don't you worry." Then he went back to polishing his Lexus.

Life, it seems, has chosen me for some strange encounters. Several times in the same year, I have been the one to hear the last words spoken by people I know, and who have left this world just as I was happening by.

The powerful spray of a hose, its nozzle turned to the

highest setting, battering the protective tarp, made me go see what was happening on the other side.

Seligman was lying in a pool of running water and detergent. His eyes were staring at the neon tube fastened to the ceiling.

I pushed aside the curtain and began massaging his heart, though I didn't know the first thing about it. A car entered the garage, and a man got out and walked towards us. It was Sedgwick. He had caught me once again, outside my job description, kneeling beside a dead man, awkwardly trying to bring him back to life, just before Shabbos fell, so he could finish the work he had started. Petrified, Sedgwick stood mute, unable to help out or take the slightest initiative. I shouted, "Do you know how to do this? Hey! Do you know or don't you?" He shook his head. I said, "Then call the ambulance. Quick, dammit!" He took out his phone and dialled a number. Then he waited, standing stock-still and useless, for someone to answer his call.

"I just saw something incredible on TV. *Beyond the Big Bang*, some kind of documentary about cosmology. You heard about that? It's really freaky. They say at the beginning of the whole thing, about three or four hundred thousand years after the Big Bang, I'm not so sure how long, I get lost in the figures like with the subprimes, but really, it doesn't matter. Anyway, after the famous explosion that blew up the universe, the sky turned cold and everything was thrown into complete darkness. Blacker than black. Can you imagine the feeling? No life, no nothing. Shit, when you think about that, you don't feel so big, and you tell yourself you've got a long way to go. Can you wrap your mind around infinity? I can't. Something that never ends, I just can't get my head around that. Everything has to have an end somewhere. We just haven't gone far enough yet. Except that when you get to the end, you've got no choice, you have to ask yourself, what's next? An end without an ending? Then you're back where you started."

Sometimes Patrick comes back from his TV-watching in a state. Generally, it happens when he watches popular-science shows, which he follows with rapt attention. He takes in the bombardment of complex information and retains only the shrapnel. Not long ago, he watched something about meteor-ology and fluid mechanics, which was illustrated, needless to say, by the image of a butterfly beating its wings, which caused a typhoon in Taipei. "The whole thing is completely crazy. After you see that, for sure, you don't know which way to go. I know it's just a way to illustrate a system, and you tell yourself that everything is going to hold together after all, but still, they shouldn't beat those wings too hard, you never know. That's what I should have done, man, if I hadn't been so stupid. I mean, study. I like learning all that stuff about the world and how storms work. It's true, when you watch that, you feel more educated. On the other hand, after you watch the Canadiens crank it up against the Bruins, you might not be any further in life, but at least you had a good time. You know what? I'm feeling so relaxed, maybe we could try cutting my hair again."

The last attempt, on the evening of Patrick's first visit to see Savage, had been a failure. It is a little like preparing for heart surgery. I set out the instruments on the shelf, and the patient takes his place on the stool. He removes his protective headscarf. The scissors enter his domain and, with their dull lips, cut down what is sticking up. When the tension gets too high, Patrick doubles over, as if he has the bends, and I stop my work. "Shit, you do that the way my mother used to. It's like you're my mother." Then, gently, imperceptibly, the blades go back to work, slipping over a strand of hair but without frightening it, easing the cutting edge into position, snipping it off without Patrick even feeling it. On the floor, the small heap of hair forms a soft mattress around the foot of his stool. I feel like I am truly accomplishing some great work, and with the same skill a mother's touch has, giving her son a new, softer look. "You did it, man. We did it. That's something big. For me, it's as powerful as the birth of the cosmos and all that shit with the butterfly. A complete haircut and I didn't even have to lie down once. The first time in my life. It's stupid, but it makes me feel like crying."

I begin cleaning up the hair on the floor. "No, no, don't touch it, I'll look after it." With meticulous care, Patrick gathers up the strands of hair and slips them into a little garbage bag. Then he ties it tightly with a string and slips it into his box of secrets hidden under his bed.

The Plane, the Tractor
and the Wait

Every aerial getaway with Winona and Nouk gave me a treasure of happiness and strength, and helped me bear the sad vicissitudes of my work. The atmosphere in the building was an ordeal, and general distrust, created by the administrator as his mandate wore on, had spread to every floor. Little by little, people began keeping an eye on each other, scrupulously enforcing every small regulation, no matter how absurd or unproductive it was. Every year, the general assembly gave rise to petty, mean-spirited speeches, wherein the owners let fly with their aggression over obviously insignificant subjects. I had to explain to the meeting the reason for this or that expense, the choice of supplier or the invoice of a service provider. People who had never set foot in a machine room started asking me about the requirements of our chlorinator, how many grams of salt per litre of water, then related the results, after useless hours on the calculator, to my overall order of sodium chloride for the season.

The beginning of the 2000s was a veritable anthology of

exercises in mediocrity, and everyone seemed eager to excel. One of the most flamboyant episodes, and probably the most ridiculous, involved candy wrappers. On several occasions during my morning rounds, I noticed the wrappers scattered through the third-floor corridors. The next day, more cellophane replaced the pieces I had picked up. It happened again the same week. I cleaned up after each day, and gave no further thought to the glutton who could have been sowing the papers. A week later, there was another harvest. This time the papers were broadcast across every floor, and even in the elevators. I decided to screen the tapes of the building's closed-circuit video system to find out who was behind the stupid joke. I was appalled at what I saw. The tapes showed Hugo Massey, a 66-year-old retiree, and his next-door neighbour Dorian West, a 58-year-old car dealer, both of whom had recently moved in, wandering around like pre-dawn ghosts, throwing their sugary papers everywhere, first on their floor, then moving on to grace every part of the building with their droppings. They engaged in their childish business every morning around 5.30 a.m., as witnessed by the tapes' time code. At that hour, they must have figured they could spread their garbage undisturbed. Think about it: this pair of old shit-heads were willing to get up before dawn to play their idiotic trick. But for what purpose? To trap me, test me, discredit me if I did not pick up after them? World's stupidest criminals: the fools forgot about the cameras, part of the security system they paid for with their monthly fees. I went to the nearest supermarket and bought two big bags of candy. I pinned a note on each one: "Thanks for the amusing videos. Signed, the janitor." Then I dropped off my presents in front of their respective doors.

From that day on, the litter disappeared from the hallways. All traces of candy-eating vanished from the surface of our little world. When we met, West and Massey greeted me with palpable embarrassment. I let it melt slowly, like a deliciously sweet dessert.

Christmas 2005. For the first time in a long time, I left the building for a week. At this period of the year, many residents would migrate south to the beaches of Cuba, Florida and Mexico. They went to soak up the dazzling sunlight that winter's drapes closed off here. Kieran Read travelled to Boston to spend the holidays with a lady friend. I never knew exactly what role she played in his life.

Winona had rented a winterised cottage for the days we were to spend together. It was perched above Fraser Lake, north of La Mauricie National Park. She borrowed a Beaver for the occasion. The plane had swapped its floats for skis so it could glide like a curling rock across the snow-covered landing strips. Watching my wife pilot the craft made my love for her grow stronger. I cherished the hours spent in the air, admiring her skill, her calm demeanour when the plane started going off in all directions, the way she had of getting it back on course, keeping track of our destination despite the wind shears, and in the end depositing Nouk and me back on the ground with all the gentleness that the rustic 1947 cabin afforded. On water or in the air, on snow or in the clouds,

Winona seemed to have the same gifts as her friend the hummingbird. She could take off in the blink of an eye and fly in all directions. Like the bird's heart, hers could adapt to the needs of the moment, speeding up with passion, slowing to do justice to reason. It was infinitely easy to love a woman like that, to share her awakening in the morning, to lie down next to her at night and feel how that magic moment marked the end of the Dark Ages. My wife was the cape, the wand, the rabbit and the hat all at once. How could the same woman pilot an airplane, love me, rescue a dog, tolerate the Excelsior, emerge from the snows and the waters, believe in the power of a bird, while giving everyone the desire to live and the taste for happiness? I had no idea.

The Christmas 2005 flight north was one of those few moments of grace we experience in the course of a lifetime. With the frigid weather, the visibility was crystal clear, and we felt we could make out the distant lands of Nunavut in an Arctic mirage. At an altitude of three thousand metres, this time of year, after the heavy snowfalls, Quebec looked like a huge pile of cotton. The countless lakes had disappeared under the ice and the snow pack. The picture was audacious in its beauty, though nearly featureless, and so uniform it made finding our way extremely difficult. I wondered what mystery made it possible for Winona to get her bearings in this enormous cake of icing sugar. Her equipment seemed rudimentary to me, more suited to visual flight than instrument navigation. But she did not seem worried at all. Sometimes she would glance back towards the tail of the plane, the way a hummingbird might do before engaging in reverse. After two and a half hours of flight, the Beaver aimed its nose downwards, then eased up on its descent and glided onto a virgin plane of white that seemed no different from any other. The plane set its skis down smoothly, leaving an imprint in the snow like a long brushstroke. When the Beaver stopped, I saw a solid log house with a smoking chimney. Nouk jumped out of the cabin and went dashing through the snow.

The inside of the house was warm and welcoming, as if the residents had just stepped out for a moment after preparing for our arrival. On a big table, a Winter White scented candle spread the smells of honey, apple and cinnamon. Such were the Christmas miracles that Winona could produce. As I entered this place with Nouk and my magic woman, I would not have been surprised if just then a small pack of wolves, the very ones that taught us to speak and stand straight in this world, had opened the door to come and share a welcome drink with us. This woman was the exception to all rules, she loved, reflected, analysed and understood this world at a glance. During the years we lived together, I never saw her face a situation she could not handle. That night, I held her in my arms until sleep came for us, while Nouk kept watch over the fire, the door, the candle and the strange sounds humans make when they indulge in eccentricities that, from her point of view, were like nothing a dog could understand.

That week slipped into our lives, eased our fatigue and dark circles, and helped us realise where we came from and what we had become. Winona was closer to her forests than I was to Skagen or the quai Lombard. Every day, she flew over her history and her territory as I grew old in the noxious greenhouse of the Excelsior. Yet I regretted nothing of this life that did not seem like very much but was enough for me.

When the weather permitted, Winona would take me and Nouk for a walk in the woods, pointing out footprints and tracks she identified with a simple glance, teaching me how to find my way in this maze of ice, and listening to the sound of the wind or the distant message of an animal. I followed her, though I did not understand everything. I moved along in her wake while Nouk, in her usual way, headed up the assembly, attentive to the silent directions my wife would give her. I loved that world, one of few words, vigilant, where intelligence could find its ancestral roots, its reflexes and observations that had preserved it in the days before there was language.

In the evening, Winona told me about her family, who had all gone their separate ways, and whom she hardly saw anymore. She spoke of the daily life of the Algonquin before the missionaries came to break down the rules and beliefs of the ancient world and sever its continuity for good. On the evening of December 24, before mass, members of several nations would gather to sing Christmas carols. "O Come, All Ye Faithful". Or "Silent Night, Holy Night".

She also told me the fabulous story of her Uncle Nathorod, known to everyone as Nate. Living in a remote region, married with three children, Nate had no choice but to follow the jobs to make money to feed his family. He worked as a miner in the Yukon, then joined the tobacco harvest, later he rented fifty hectares and grew crops and raised animals, but all that was not enough. He hired on as a truck driver with a haulage company that ran between Toronto and Vancouver. The trip had to be completed in five days, which left very little time for rest. When he retired, Nate turned in the keys to his Mack and went back to his family. By then he was feeling old, and he knew his time was all the more precious, for he could imagine the end. One morning, he knew the day had come.

Winona's voice slowly opened the doors of this story, one after the other. "My uncle got the whole family together and told them, 'I've been working for you all my life. And that's OK. But now I'm an old man and I've decided to do something for myself, and myself alone. I've decided to drive my old tractor across Canada, from the Pacific to the Atlantic. Eight thousand kilometres on my old John Deere. It'll take as long as it takes.' Nate had a friend drive his tractor to Horseshoe Bay, just outside Vancouver. He backed the machine up to the water's edge, and dipped his rear wheels into the Pacific Ocean. Then he started off, heading east. For four months, at ten or fifteen kilometres an hour, whatever the weather, he drove along to see, as he put it, 'What the roads and the men of this country are like, but also, before I die, I want to do something nobody else has ever done.' Along the way he had all kinds of adventures and misadventures. When he reached the far end of the continent, in Saint John's, Newfoundland, my uncle stopped with his front wheels touching the Atlantic. Then he got an idea, unexpected, but essential. He did not want anyone to question his word, so he asked someone to attest to what he had witnessed, and sign the document and date it. Though they were of no importance to anyone else, those papers were the most memorable and precious things in his life. He often mentioned the famous witness, Mr

Hautshing, I remember the name perfectly. Many years later, he took me to his garage, where he had parked his old partner John Deere, and lifted a tarp from a shelf. He showed me two cans of water. On one was written in big letters 'Pacific Ocean' and on the other 'Atlantic Ocean'. He lifted those two jerrycans and said, 'I filled the both of them up at both ends of the country.' His eyes filled with tears. And that's the story of my Uncle Nate's journey."

I imagined Winona closing a big picture book, the kind of marvellous tale we read to children so they will have sweet dreams. It was certainly the most touching, moving and instructive tale I had ever heard.

"Do you know what happened the day he was buried? He made a request before his death. Once his coffin was lowered into the ground, his children stepped up to the grave and emptied the two cans into it."

The fire burned low. Now and then, the crackle of a pine log would breathe new life into it. Outside, the snowstorm that was predicted had begun. Winona put on her anorak and her fur boots, then disappeared into the night, a dark figure surrounded by white squalls, to make sure the Beaver was safely tied up. She gauged how much snow had fallen, and then slowly, as if she wanted to stay outside longer to enjoy the storm, she came back to our house. Nouk appeared and stuck her nose under my arm. As she went past, Winona kissed me, then left me to converse with her Uncle Nate, who held high the ocean waters that had one day parted to let him pass through dry-shod.

. . .

"It won't be long before my trial starts up, and I want to get your opinion. Do you think I'd be smarter to plead guilty? Now don't go thinking I did anything wrong. I'm innocent now, more than ever. But I know judges, they're twisted in the head, and I figured you might have some ideas. I don't mean that you're twisted in the head, too, but since you're so smart, you can calculate things before they happen and all that, so I figured you might have an opinion."

My deep-seated conviction is that Patrick sent his friend the informer *ad patres*, and now he is looking for a way out of a bad situation in which he played the role he chose to. "With a guilty plea, can a guy admit a little bit, but not all of it? Let me explain. The way things happened with the dead man, OK, I was hanging out with him. I knew he was a snitch, OK. And it so happened that I punched out his lights. So far, no problem. But then, stop. What happens next, I had nothing to do with. By the time he gets the 9 mm in the head, I'm nowhere to be seen. I might as well have been at home. A good ten minutes by car. So how can I be a suspect? That's where the business of the half-guilty plea comes in, just for the stuff at the beginning. Do they have that in court, do you think, a half-guilty plea?"

In view of what Patrick showed me from his file and the testimony it contains, I think that "a half-guilty plea", a concept that is new to me as far as the justice system is concerned, would constitute fucking contempt of court, to use Patrick's language.

"Except for a couple of bullshit things, I don't think they have much against me. If I make them an offer, I'm giving them a way out, and that's what my lawyer always says to do. He tells me, Mr Horton, you always have to give the judge a way out, or else he's going to turn against you in a hurry. So getting back to my offer, it's give and take, I admit I did some shit and the judge sentences me to time served. We shake hands and part friends, regards to the folks! What do you think? In my opinion, it'll work. Especially when you know that, except for a couple of punches, I'm completely innocent."

Patrick is having one of his bad days, a bad run when all sorts of parasitic ideas and thoughts begin to take over his mind, impairing his judgement and what remains of his common sense. When he gets like that, it is better for him to blow off steam, and for me to wait for the pressure to ease off. I should have followed that protocol myself, that day at the Excelsior, when my life took a wrong turn. When I stood before the judge, I did not even have the presence of mind to plead "half-guilty".

The beginning of 2006 truly was an ordeal. As Kieran Read had predicted, after a few years of tuning up, the cost killer was hitting his stride, checking here, cutting there, generating useless addenda to the pages of the rules and procedures, which, since he had been elected president, had swelled to the size of a telephone book. We were not living in a building anymore, but a despotic principality where the prince was in charge of everything. The most surprising thing was how the residents willingly submitted to the whims of the little monarch. Meanwhile, I was the designated whipping boy, being the front-line subject whose responsibilities included spending the royal treasury. Sedgwick was a compulsive memo writer, and he criticised me in writing for buying too much salt for the swimming pool, too many cleaning products, not following to the letter the manufacturer's recommendations concerning the lawnmower maintenance schedule, setting the thermostat too high on the pool's heating system, even if the temperature had been set by the board of directors themselves, not taking out the garbage early enough, bringing the cans back in too late, neglecting to keep my dog on a leash in the hallway when I took her out for a walk. I felt so belittled when I received these notes that I hid them from Winona and did not mention them to Kieran. I think Sedgwick was "calculating things before they happened", as Patrick put it. He had planned his strategy from the start, which was to get me to resign and replace me with service providers.

My maintenance and repair work had long been a source of satisfaction. I felt a craftsman's pride in a job well done. But now I was just following procedures blindly, with no real thought. I had nothing to say to anyone anymore as I obeyed the guidebook, head down, though it was leading the principality towards its decline.

I stopped responding to personal requests that were "outside the scope of my job description". The condo owners offered me money to do small repairs, which I used to do for free. Now I turned them away and referred them to a repairman. Often they took my refusal badly, as a personal affront. I had once been an affable chamberlain under the reign of

Alexandre, but now I was a sullen concierge under Sedgwick's regime. I did not know it yet, but at the beginning of that year, the countdown had begun for me.

But all that was nothing compared to the misfortune that would destroy part of me for ever. It is still as unbearable today as it was on the first day. On the evening of the tragedy, it was strange, but the only person I thought of who I needed to take me in his arms was my father Johanes Hansen, the pastor whose name I bear. That evening, I remember asking him outright, in a way I had never done while he was alive, "Papa, this time, help me." I didn't know if anything could be done, I was hoping for a miracle to save us from disaster, a voice that would tell us it was alright, nothing had happened, now we could all go home, sit down to dinner together, then turn off the memories and the lights of a bad day.

On Saturday, August 12, 2006, Winona woke up early. I don't remember if she kissed me the way she usually did when she left before me. She had an eight o'clock appointment at the floatplane base to fly three fishermen and their gear to the shores of Lake Mistassini, near Chibougamau, a two-and-a-half-hour flight to a point north-east of Montreal. Her plane took off at 9 a.m. from the Rivière des Prairies. As it did every time, the Beaver got airborne with men aboard happy to be among their fellows, carrying with them extra testosterone and enough beer and live bait to impress the fish.

The day passed and night came. If the coverage was good, Winona would call and tell me when she was about to take off, what the weather looked like, and what time she would be home. Around 8 p.m., there was still no news. I called Pradier, the Beav'Air manager. He told me he was waiting for the plane, and had no information.

Night fell, lighting up the tall buildings of the city by the river in their summer apparel. To the west, the last fires of the setting sun, and here, at my window, the embers of anguish. There was no plausible reason why Winona had not returned. She should have been back around 5 p.m. If she had not contacted anyone, something must have happened to prevent her. At 10 p.m., Pradier called me and reported that he had managed to reach one of the fishermen, who confirmed that Winona had dropped them off at noon, then taken off from the lake again, heading for Montreal, at 1.30 p.m. "I think I'll have to call for a search," Pradier said.

I spent the night in darkness, on the couch, clutching the phone in one hand, Nouk pressed against my side. For the first time, she barely touched her evening meal. The steam-roller of hours advanced pitilessly, and crushed all remaining hope I might have. When daylight entered our house, I knew Winona was dead, it was over, my wife would never come back to me, this time the hummingbird had lost the power of its wings. At one point the telephone would ring and a voice would say, "Are you Mr Hansen?" What that voice would say next would be absolutely irrelevant.

Kieran had heard the reports on the TV news, and came to share my waiting. He did not speak much. He made coffee, and we sipped at it quietly.

A helicopter and a military aircraft patrolled the flight corridor that the plane was supposed to have taken. With no results. On Monday, a powerful summer thunderstorm with high winds interrupted the search. I left the apartment to let the dog out, then we returned to our cave to hide our pain and fear. Nouk scarcely ate anything. She was usually so full of life and energy, but now, already, she seemed to be wearing an invisible cloak of mourning. She would not leave my side, not for her reassurance, but to comfort me. I tucked my fingers into her thick fur, squeezed her chest and felt her heart beating against my hands. All I could do was bury my face in her coat, and tell her I loved her, and cry. I knew Winona was dead. She had disappeared when the Beaver fell from the sky and crashed. Her body was trapped in the plane at the bottom of a lake. Or had been charred when the cabin exploded. I did not want to know the circumstances, because then the slow reconstruction of the tragedy would begin, with the avalanche of questions about the state of her remains. Her face torn apart, her flesh made unrecognisable, her bones shattered, the invisible black boxes of the mind that could never reconstruct the words and thoughts, the fury, panic and pain of the final seconds when she began to understand, even before the point of impact, that now the man and the dog belonged to the other world, the one where you have to comfort yourself with nonsense tales about the power of birds, the patience of wolves, the benevolence of the gods, the training of church rabbits and even the solidity of airplanes, even if everyone has always known that they "have a reputation for being unpredictable, and no advance signs prepare the pilot for a stall. The shock is sudden, and at low altitude, it is often very difficult to right the craft, which may lead to a fatal outcome."

I did not want to think about those things. I did not

want that mass of questions invading me, that flood of useless hypotheses and technical terms set end to end, glued together to outwit my waiting with a makeshift wall hastily built between me and the impending news. Because everyone knows that when the time comes, that news will sweep away this meagre defence with a single word.

The information arrived on Thursday in the early afternoon. The doorbell rang. Two members of the Royal Canadian Mounted Police.

"I am here to report on the status of the search. The wreckage of the aircraft was located this morning at approximately 8.30 a.m. near Cedar Island on Lake Kempt, an hour's flight from Montreal. Apparently, the plane attempted an emergency landing, but it did not go well. Teams are on site to recover your wife's body. Unfortunately, she did not survive. We will come for you once we have brought her back to Montreal. We are very sorry. Saddened, and sorry for your loss."

The two policemen stood before me. I tried to speak, but could not. Something had escaped me and was fleeing, full speed straight ahead, something I had kept in me since childhood, no doubt a part of myself that has never returned. I looked at the policemen. I put out my right hand in their direction. I felt the weight of the world crushing me, and with no strength left in my legs to hold me up, I slowly collapsed at their feet.

At the morgue, I think everyone had done their best to help me recognise Winona's mutilated body. They showed me her tortured face and then no more. I did not look away, I stood by her a moment so that every part of what misfortune had given

·me would be engraved on my heart, and when it was about to explode, I walked out.

Kieran did his best. He managed to find a distant member of Winona's family, and the man came to see me. He introduced himself as a vague cousin on her father's side. We knew nothing about each other, and had nothing to say, except the essentials.

"Winona Mapachee was the daughter of my father's second brother. We went to school together, then we lost track of each other. When we found out what happened, my old man said, 'Go down there and ask the man if he'll let us bring this child's body back to her land, so we can bury her here at home.' That's what he told me. I've come to make this request."

I don't know what my wife would have wanted. Nothing is more futile than trying to think for the dead. So I let my heart speak and it said yes, you can bring her home to be among her people. But I will not make the journey north. I will leave it to you to drive her, prepare her and celebrate her in the darkness of the grave. I will even leave you her bird, and you will put it in with her. I will keep everything else. The eleven years of happiness and all its riches, eleven years I feasted on from heaven and on earth, with the incredible daughter of your father's second brother. She was the person I always tried to stand straight for, in the snow of the forests, through the summers and the storms. Everywhere I followed her. She knew how to reveal the best in everyone. I will leave you her body broken by the plane, but I am keeping everything else. To each his inheritance. It is a terrible thing to share. Drive carefully.

During the week that followed the discovery of the crash

site, I remained cloistered in my apartment. I did not give the Excelsior a thought, not for a single second. None of the residents knocked at my door. No-one came to call. To take my mind off things, Kieran told me that Sedgwick had posted a new addendum to the rules governing the conduct of deck-chairs, "which after use must never be left on the grassy areas".

The humid air came creeping in. Winona was certainly in the ground by then. I could not bear the thought. There were times I wanted to jump in the car and drive north and take her back from her family. Other times, I imagined her going in peace among her people and the spirit of her ancestors, telling them, among other things, that where she could discern eighty kinds of snow, the white man could see only "accumulations".

Nouk walked in my footsteps, and if she had been able to, she would have lived inside me. We went out at night for long walks through the streets, then to Ahuntsic Park. When the temperature was stifling and the air dripping with humidity, as is often the case this time of year, the dog would run ahead and stop at the edge of the big pond. She would stare at me with her black eyes that clearly asked, "Can I go in?" I walked up to her, stroked her attentive face and answered, "By all means!" Nouk leaped into the water and swam from one end to the other as if, somewhere in this pool, a drowning man's life depended on it. In those fleeting moments, she and I felt exactly the same thing, that in us, if only for a few minutes, a little joy and happiness might return.

Return to Skagen

At the excelsior, every hour, every working day became a burden. I continued to go up to the roof, carry out my inspections, listen to my rotors and weigh my salt on the precision scale the way it is done in the backrooms of haute cuisine. With his usual insistence, Sedgwick palpated my ledger of expenses, codifying and appending his notes. Kieran Read had retired, and now he spent more evenings with me, and would try to tow me out to an Indian restaurant or the latest Argentine film. But I knew no true peace until I found myself with Nouk, who greeted me every time I came back as if I had just returned from a faraway expedition.

I sometimes thought of Mr Seligman, and wondered if somewhere in the city there was a synagogue where you could improve your skills as a widower, the way it was said a person could for golf or tennis, a synagogue where the rabbi would stick to dispensing my friend Patrick's basic philosophy: "Life is like an old nag. If she throws you off, shut up and climb back on again."

Against all expectations, in 2007, work was what helped me

straighten out, win back a little dignity and fight Sedgwick's authoritarian delirium. During the winter, after a Lord's Day spent bent over and labouring in the basement, I succeeded in reconnecting the entire building's hot-water supply. And in the dog days of August, after seventy-two hours of measurement and constant adjustments, I saved the sixty-eight owners' pool party and with it the two hundred and thirty thousand litres of water, sentenced to the sewers a few days earlier by the company that managed the new system's maintenance. In the space of a few months, to the great dismay of the man who thought he was through with me, I became the miracle worker again, a sort of Edward Scissorhands who could trim hedges into topiaries, discipline the plumbing and all but walk on water.

But in the evening, when I returned to my apartment, my reality took a rough hold on me again. My door opened onto an interior that had been empty since August 12, 2006. I made something to eat, then Nouk and I, side by side, shared the same meal in our respective bowls.

The winter of 2008 was one of the snowiest on record in this part of the country. In Quebec City, two and a half metres of snow fell, and the same was true for Montreal. Some days, I ran the little snow blower twice to clear the entryway and the other approaches to the Excelsior. To check on my extractors on the roof, I had to dig tunnels through the heaps of snow, necessary pathways that had to be cleared each morning with a shovel. The only one who enjoyed the incessant snowfalls was Nouk. In Ahuntsic Park, she forgot all about the wading pool and rolled in the mountains of virgin snow, sometimes disappearing into them, then shook herself free and ran off to the next drift.

That year, the summer was one of excess as well, when it came to temperature and humidity. At night, the city simmered under a cover, slowly baking along with our vapours and our moods. The entire second half of August belonged to the Dog Star, and Kieran Read decided to go into exile with a Boston lady friend who had a house on Rexhame Beach. Sometimes he would call me as evening fell, and the simple sound of his voice carried with it a cool breeze of ocean air.

One night, at the end of my rope, suffocating in my small ground-floor flat, I slipped on my bathing suit. With everyone asleep at two o'clock in the morning, I made my way to the pool whose lights had been doused.

I eased into the water. It was my water, and I had kept it afloat and refurbished all these years, my water treated with salt, electrolysed, filtered and maintained at a perfect pH. I had spent endless days and nights keeping watch over it, the guardian of its biological balance and ideal temperature, 84.2 degrees Fahrenheit. I entered that water as if it were my domain. I felt it encircle my waist, then cover my shoulders and back, embrace my neck and submerge my head. I had been working here for more than twenty years, and this was the first time I had trespassed onto this territory of wonders that was forbidden to me. I swam underwater, holding my breath, enjoying this bath of miracles. I loved the water and felt that it loved me, too. Its "texture", as Mr Sibelius often pointed out, was light, almost airy, as if oxygenated by an infinity of microscopic bubbles. I surfaced for air, then dived down again to the depths where I had so often carried out my work. For the first time in all these years, I transgressed the rule. And it was wonderful. I did not know how long I had spent in the pool, but when I pulled myself onto the deck, I remember cursing that damned Sedgwick and his pettiness for having deprived Winona of this pleasure during the years she lived here. What that cost-killing little drill sergeant could not have known was that, all summer, depending on where her travels took her, while he stood guard at the foot of the building on the lookout for infractions like a modern Cerberus, my wife, immersed in her world, swam in the country's wildest and most beautiful lakes.

Back in the apartment, I took Nouk out with me to cool her down in the waters of the footbath. Then we both fell asleep, refreshed, content, like two little thieves after a long night's work.

Two days later, I received a call from Sedgwick. "Paul, weren't you supposed to meet a supplier tomorrow morning? Call him and cancel. I want to see you in the meeting room tomorrow at ten. I have called an extraordinary session of the board of directors and owners to make a decision on a rule that concerns you. Tomorrow, 10 a.m."

Not a single person was missing. Every floor was represented. Every door. Singles, couples, a mix of ages and generations. Sedgwick was presiding, flanked by his two assessors, who would have laid down their bodies for him. "Good morning to everyone. This meeting concerns a point in the main rules and regulations that our superintendent Paul Hansen has violated. During the night between Tuesday and Wednesday, around two o'clock in the morning, despite the fact that his contract expressly forbids him to do so, Mr Hansen, unknown to all, swam in our pool. The surveillance videos make this clear. And as if this lack of respect was not sufficient, he returned several moments after his swim with his dog, and immersed it in the footbath." Like an icy blast of winter air, a disapproving hubbub ran through the room. The public humiliation had produced its desired effect. In his civil servant's language, Sedgwick pursued the inquisition. "By doing so, Mr Hansen, you have committed a serious professional breach, unilaterally broken your contract and, most of all, abused the trust that all of us here have placed in you. By immersing your dog in our footbath, you ignored the basic hygiene measures that I set down concerning the use of the pool, and put the owners in this room at risk. For all these reasons that, contractually, now make you unable to carry out your tasks, I am asking today that your employment be terminated. Such termination will come into effect at the end of the month of September. At that time, you will receive what is owed you, and in turn you will surrender the keys to your apartment. Before putting this motion to a vote, do you have anything to say, Mr Hansen?" As often happened in my father's churches, a murmur was heard from the little crowd. No-one could say if it was an expression of compassion, or the grumbling of disapproval.

What could a person say, how could he answer or add anything after hearing such things, a litany of charges spun from the finest threads of small-mindedness? More than twenty years of loyal service, hours of work past all measure, a form of serfdom on every floor, the life of the garden, the battle with the water, the campaign against winter, the candy wrappers, helping out the sick, bringing the dying back to life, giving extreme unction, burying the dead – all forgotten because of a midnight swim.

From the back of the room a voice rose up. It belonged to Johanes, from his finest hours, the voice that brought miners up from the pits, speaking louder and stronger and longer than the explosions in the mines, yelling into the horses' ears on the racetrack, the voice that had attended to my birth and my growing years and had never let me down. It was still here today to take up the sword, cut stupidity, ignorance and pettiness down to size, beat the idiot, strike the rule-bound and draw me from the waters.

I wish Kieran Read had been there that day. That he had returned from Boston. He, too, would have led the charge against the multitudes, attacking them from every angle. But there was no battle, not even an attempt at self-defence. Unanimity less four votes gave me thirty days to jam my memories, my dog and my few remaining shreds of dignity into a moving van. I exited the room without speaking a word. My brain was locked, it would not produce anything intelligible, except a terrible and secret feeling of shame. That day, like the taste of black bile, a sentence lingered in my mouth, it said what it had to say, then began again, repeating. It issued from a history book my father owned in which a Catholic bishop known for his contempt, referring to the resistance of the petty clergy, advised an alter ego to run roughshod over the lower members of the cloth. "You'll see, the human being is a docile creature."

At the end of the meeting, Sedgwick said to me, "You know, Paul, there is nothing personal in any of this, there are rules we all have to respect and follow. I am sure you understand." Then he left with his Praetorian Guard to bring order to some other court, elsewhere, in his world of border patrols and clerks charged with expelling, consigning and punishing all janitors and their midnight summer swims.

Because such is my nature, I continued carrying out the maintenance chores. In the evening, I packed my boxes. Nouk wondered what was going on. She would sniff them, one after the other, a worried look on her face.

One very humid afternoon, I was finishing up mowing a section of the lawn when Sedgwick came striding up in my direction. He was clearly beside himself. My ear protection kept me from hearing the beginning of his rant. But what followed was as clear as a bell. "How many times do I have to say the same thing before you'll understand, Hansen? What do you have between your ears? We fired you for professional misconduct, and three days later you're back at it again. Are you an idiot, or what?" No doubt I was, since I had put up with this man for so long. A double idiot, because I had no idea what could have provoked such a storm of anger. "Look where your dog is, Hansen! Lying in the grass! By the maples!" Indeed, Nouk was under the trees, stretched out in the shade, in the greenery, trying to get a breath of fresh air. She must have followed me, then neglected to read the rules and regulations, the sub-paragraphs governing the lives of humans, and their animals as well. In his rage, Sedgwick said something that stirred the education I had received from the wolves. "Get that goddamned animal out of here! I don't want to see it in this building one more second! You get it? Get out of here, both of you, now!" That is when the wolves showed me the way. I leaped on the administrator, knocked him down and dragged him to the edge of the pool. I know I hit him hard, and kept hitting him, going for every part I could reach, with the savage mind of the pack; I felt or heard the sound of two bones breaking, and I didn't let up, I bit him on the shoulder, deep enough to come away with a piece of flesh. I had a piece of Sedgwick in my mouth and it had no taste at all, just the nauseating odour of bad blood. I heard his screams, he was asking for something I could not give him anymore, pity or some equivalent that you can find in the manuals of piety. He was begging me but I didn't know for what, calling for help most likely, from his guards, his army, but no-one showed up. I dragged him to the water and together, like two swimmers at play, we tipped into the pool. He was struggling and his hair went this way and that like algae swept by the current. I was slowly drowning him and watched him through the blur of my water, which was eager to pour into his lungs and drive out every molecule of air for ever. On the surface, figures came and went, and I heard Nouk's muffled barking with the other wolves of the pack. Time lost all reality and consistence, nothing was left but

214

the texture of the water and the blood flowing from the bite I inflicted on our master's shoulder. He was struggling the way animals that still want to live do, when humans want to drown them because they do not want them around anymore. For years now, though I did not realise it until then, I had been running circles in the depths of this pathogenic building that had slowly dispossessed me of all I had. And now, the master and I were swimming in the same water forbidden to me, mano-a-mano, wolf against wolf, with just enough air in our lungs to hold on to life for a few more seconds, those precious moments we await and fear all our lives, those last instants that end up disappointing us, revealing only the faulty perspectives of the Horton Theorem, for once the infinite time of drowning has passed, nothing, absolutely nothing, begins again.

Above me, bodies splashed into the water, grabbed my arms, took hold of me and freed Sedgwick from my grasp. They dragged me out of the water and onto the ground, and kept me there. I fought like an animal caught in a trap, screaming with pain and rage. A moment later, everything went black.

I woke up the next day in a hospital room reserved for patients in police custody. A doctor came and gave me my bill of health, and a little later, an investigator informed me of Sedgwick's state. Two broken arms, a broken finger, a shoulder bite causing loss of skin, multiple contusions of the thorax, multiple injuries to the face requiring twenty-one stitches. "The judge will decide, when he hears the witnesses, whether you will be accused of attempted murder by drowning. When you recover, you will be transferred to Bordeaux Prison."

It was mid-September. I had suffered a concussion, which meant I was under the standard protocol, and had undergone surgery to the lumbar region. Both conditions kept me in bed and under observation, in this special part of the hospital, until the end of October. Kieran Read was informed, and he returned from Boston after the event to look after Nouk, who had been locked in my apartment after the incident. Both had visited me several times.

On November 4, in the morning, I stood before Judge Lorimier.

"As for the assault and battery charges, I believe there is no sense wasting time. On the other hand, I would like to question you about the way you continued your violent actions underwater, since your fight ended up at the bottom of a swimming pool, which is quite unusual, and it took six people to make you let go. During the final exchange of blows, when you and your adversary were underwater, without oxygen, were you truly intending to drown Mr Sedgwick, or was this last part of the battle just the submarine version of what had begun on dry land?" I answered his strange questions by telling him I could not answer, I did not remember much, I was unable to judge my true intentions because I could not re-enact the events. "Six people. Six people to pry you off Mr Sedgwick. Six. And according to their testimony, they had to fight you like the devil. And the bite. Six by five centimetres of flesh ripped away. Do you understand? I have seen your file, you have had no run-ins with the law, your professional life is exemplary, your family respectable, your father was a pastor in Thetford Mines, and I also see that besides your French citizenship, you have acquired a Canadian passport. What went through your mind? You refused to tell police anything about your conflict with your employer. Would you like to do better with me?"

There are some things a man is better off keeping to himself. Or sharing only with his wife, his father and his dog. And the ones who know the story from its very beginning, buried somewhere beneath the sands of Skagen, are not in a position to judge.

Despite my lawyer's wandering approximations owing to a mind floating on Prozac, Lorimier dismissed the charges of attempted murder and sentenced me to two years with no possibility of parole. That very evening, as Barack Obama was raising his arms in triumph, I entered my cell in Bordeaux Prison with bowed head.

One evening a year ago, Savage called me to his office. Kieran Read had informed him that Nouk had died. A fulminating disease of the liver. Whose name he had forgotten.

This time nothing was left, no family, no freedom, no dog. I cried in front of the man who loved motorcycles. Everything had happened outside of me, away from me, and worst of all I had not been there, at the very end, when I knew she would have sought out the crook of my arm and burrowed her nose there.

I asked Savage if I could attend my dog's cremation.

He answered no.

I asked Savage if I could keep her ashes in my cell.

He answered no.

I asked Savage if he would request that Kieran Read keep them.

He answered, "That's up to you to arrange."

Back in my cell, Nouk's death awoke the memory of the many disappearances that had marked my life over these last years. The thought that I had let my dog go all by herself broke my heart, and stripped away my sense of propriety. I dissolved in tears right in front of Patrick Horton. First he was intrigued. He bent his head to the right, then to the left, and moved cautiously towards me, observing with a worried look. Then awkwardly he reached out his arms in my direction, the way a person would who wanted to soothe a crying baby, but did not know how to go about it.

"It's going to be fucking weird. I hope they're not going to replace you with the priest that ate up those little boys. You know who I mean, the guy we talked about the other day, that bishop who did his shopping at the parish summer camp. Twelve metres tall and a hatchet face, remember? Do you realise, you got parole, and you didn't even want to talk to your evaluator? Which proves that those guys are like tits on a bull, completely useless. You're something else, man, I'm telling you, I'm going to miss you. You promised to stay in touch, don't forget. And if you get any info about my idea of pleading half-guilty, you remember, right, let me know what you think. Now you better get going, otherwise they'll send you back to the condo, you know that. I want you to forget about the guy you put in a sling, and get on with your life. I know what's going to happen next. And I also know the first thing you're going to do when you get out of here. You want me to tell you? Nine guys out of ten, when they leave here, an hour later they're on Sainte-Catherine Street, or out in Hochelaga, getting their rocks off. But the only thing you've got in your head is to go and get your dog's ashes. Am I right, or am I right?"

Parked on Gouin Boulevard, close by the river and not far from the floatplane base, Kieran was waiting for me, sitting on the fender of his car. When he saw me, he walked up and put his arms around me. In my hand, the canvas bag with all my worldly goods. My apartment had been emptied and the furniture sold off to the highest bidder by a sort of liquidator hired to clear the place out.

"You're going to come and stay at the house a while, Paul. The apartment is big enough, and it's all set up for you."

It did not take long to get to the Excelsior, a few minutes at most. It was the beginning of July, a splendid summer. At first it was not easy to get out of the car, find the courage to walk through my garage, step into the lift, climb the floors in the silence of the cables, breathe in the strong smell of the corridors, stare at the garden gone to ruin, and spot the little imperfections around the swimming pool.

In two years, all sorts of little things had changed. I was not at home anymore. The building had not recognised me.

Nouk's ashes were waiting on the bookshelf in the bedroom Kieran prepared for me. They did not take up much room. I asked him if he had personally attended the cremation. "From the beginning to the end, you can rest assured. That's Nouk, she's all there." When he left the room, I picked up the urn in my hands and held it close to my side.

When evening fell, Kieran took me out to eat in a restaurant he had discovered on Van Horne Avenue. He told me how my dog had fallen ill, and described how he had stayed by her until the very last moment. Then he switched over to the building, how the costs had risen, and conflicts broken out, the failings of my replacement, and Edouard Sedgwick's declining star. "I have a question for you, Paul. I have been thinking about it since you left. In the job I do, you know, I have seen a lot of strange things. But this is the first time, I assure you, that I witnessed a guy break both arms of the person he was fighting at the same time, in one move. Two complete fractures. How did you manage that magic trick?" I had never considered the issue in that light. I could not supply a worthy answer to the man across from me. But on the way back to the apartment, I understood that Kieran was much more interested in the fractures, which were a completely common injury, than in the fact that I had ripped away a good piece of Sedgwick's shoulder with my teeth.

The subject of conversation filled the entire next day. And the day after that. He thought I would be running a needless risk. I considered it the first step in my integration back into society. Since I was no longer the building's superintendent, I could enjoy my new status as a guest, which gave me the privilege, with Kieran's authorisation, of course, of swimming two or three lengths in the pool as Sedgwick looked on. Then I would bask in the sun a minute or two on one of the lawn chairs, after which I would put my robe back on and go upstairs, my head held high and my spirit finally cleansed and freed of all the nights of anger and hatred that had burdened it.

The day was ideal for the exercise. A scorching end to the afternoon with a staggering humidex rating, the hour when wasps came to drink and owners refreshed their evil thoughts from the past while seeking reasons to secrete new ones. The hour when every pair of swim trunks concealed a raging demon. An hour that was forbidden to me, as all other hours were. Why? Because. The hour of expensive sunscreen, when martinis smelled like the endgame, when the oldest clung to their floating lives.

We arrived side by side through the main entrance. It was impossible not to see us. Two robes, blindingly white. I passed my shirt to Kieran, who went to recline on a chaise longue.

I moved past the footbath and, slowly, step by step, entered the water. Before diving beneath its surface, I gazed upon the perfect world around me, the horizontal alignment of condo owners in order of size and importance. All those who had driven me out were present, oiled and pink like old meat. From my perspective, they all appeared tiny.

Sedgwick was positioned in the middle, the centre, at the very heart of his principality. The consul's face was waxen, and he was wearing a nasty scar on his shoulder. He, too, seemed very small, "a quantity of no importance whatsoever", as Johanes used to say. No-one spoke to me. Every eye stared in my direction as if I had become some sort of magnetic north, as if suddenly the world's axis had tilted. I listened to the perfection of that silence for another moment, then dove into the depths of the pool. I stayed underwater as long as I could, so that everyone would think they had actually seen my ghost that had been swallowed up by the pool, which dissolved it with its salt before flushing it down the proper channels. When my lungs were about to explode, I emerged from the water like a rorqual surfacing for air, then dived back to the depths again. I had shaved, better to feel the water's caress on my face. The water hardly touched me at all. Its texture had changed, but it had done its job, cleansing my spirit, filtering out the impurities. Three or four times, I disappeared, only to return again. As I left the stage, I contemplated all those poor actors who were trying to stay in character, and play their supporting roles. I swam towards the pool's edge and grabbed on to it. Floating between land and sea, in the strategic position of a prone marksman, I stared at Edouard Sedgwick. The way you might look at a dead animal. The cure that consisted in silent observation must have seemed endless to him, but he did not turn away as I enjoyed the delicious spectacle of his broken pride and wounded shoulder.

When I felt my heart reach a state of peace, I emerged slowly from the water, step by step. In the grass, her ears telling of her happiness, her tail joyful, I saw Nouk, my dog, waiting for me.

As I stretched out on the chaise longue next to Kieran, I heard him say, "You had me on the edge of my seat. You were like an orca playing Marineland."

A few moments later, Sedgwick left his spot and made a wide detour to avoid crossing paths with us. Seeing him retreating so ingloriously, Kieran spoke. "You know what, Paul? At the end of the year I'm going to run against him."

I spent a dozen days or so in Montreal, getting used to life on the outside. I went to Indigo and bought three books. *Harley-Davidson: The Complete History*, *Harley-Davidson: An Illustrated Guide* and *Art of the Harley-Davidson Motorcycle*.

I had no idea how many years Patrick might spend behind bars, but with this literature, he would have a means of escape, right in front of the guards. And, why not, there just might be some exchange value with Emmanuel Savage. As for me, I had decided to enjoy my freedom and travel to Denmark. I had no idea how long I might stay. My itinerary began with the sky: Montreal to Geneva to Copenhagen. Next, the ferry, and then the road, via Aarhus, Randers and Aalborg, right to the very top of the peninsula, and Skagen.

To give me time and space to get organised for this long voyage, Kieran was kind enough to leave me his apartment and travel to Boston. He called me every evening. He was afraid of an incident, and made me promise not to go back to the pool until he returned. I had no reason to. What needed to be done was done.

Then came the last thing I wanted to accomplish. The day before my departure, I took a taxi to Île Notre-Dame and the giant casino there that Johanes had never known. The open secret known as the Money Maker, the place that caused his downfall, had disappeared. In its place stood the new casino, an imposing machinery of chance, a factory of destiny that, twenty-four hours a day and seven days a week, recycled the variables of luck and clipped the wings of chance.

I climbed the great staircase under a cascade of lights. Gamblers for one evening, or for all eternity, prowled the tables, moved by ambitions that were surely unreasonable, each one believing in that little inner glow that would never flicker out. They were convinced that it would happen, one day or another, because they had waited their whole lives for it and thought they were deserving. *Muss es sein? Es muss sein.*

Nouk, with Johanes and Winona on either side of her, was waiting for me by a roulette table. Together, they were the most living dead in this world. The most faithful, the most adventurous. They had endured Patrick's lower intestines and the belly of the prison, the cold cells and the slow days. On this island, this workshop of defeat, they had surprised me once again. They knew long before I did that I would start my journey here, to avenge Johanes in my way, to pay off his accounts, wipe the slate clean, and put the figures in good order.

We spent quite some time, the four of us, letting the wheel turn on its wooden table, watching the ball waltzing across the copper dial, as men of goodwill pushed their chips around. They hoped to come out ahead by betting on inside or outside, straight or single, corner or square, six line or double street, top line or basket, red or black. Misfortune offered a whole gamut of variables and colours.

My father had tried them all, mixed and mashed them

until there was nothing left, until, one night, a woman took his face in her hands, kissed him, and told him softly, "If he sees you, may God bless you."

I felt good. I gazed upon my loved ones. I felt their hearts beating and I breathed their breath. I felt at peace with them. They were protecting my life, all three in their own way. I wanted them to know how much I loved them.

When the croupier called, "Place your bets," I put one hundred dollars' worth of chips on black and left the room. As I went, I heard him say, "Last bets." When the final announcement was made, "No more bets, *rien ne va plus*," I was already walking along the river, leaving the croupier to make sense of the rest.

Yesterday, with the ashes of my dog, I gave myself plenty of time for checking in. The stopover at Geneva Cointrin. The long hours of waiting to change worlds.

Then Copenhagen Kastrup, the boat, the road along the dunes that narrowed as it reached the tip of the peninsula.

The brisk air, the sharp light, the separation of the currents, the meeting of the seas. Skagen.

The hotel. Sleep awaiting lorazepam. Evil thoughts, infinitely patient, coming and going in the room.

Then daybreak, like in the paintings, the delicate illumination of men and boats, dunes and waves.

I walk along the street bordering the sea. It is called Østre Strandvej, the oyster road. In the distance, I spot the big house that belongs to the Hansens, the one with the red roof. The house faces the Baltic. The wind bends the trees and whips the sand that piles up against the buildings.

I breathe in the sea air of this new country. It is all I have now.

Soon, at the end of this long road, I will greet my family. I will knock on the front door, someone will open it, and as my father taught me, I will say, *"Hej, søn ag Johanes Hansen."*

I am the son of Johanes Hansen.

Acknowledgements

M Y DEEPEST THANKS to Serge Asselin for his generous help and precious expertise.

With all my affection for Geneviève, Claire and Didier.

I would also like to express my gratitude to Aurélie, Laurence, Lydie, Virginie and Pierre, and also to Jeanne, Nathalie K., Nathalie P., Pauline, Violaine, Clément and, of course, Olivier. They welcomed me to Éditions de l'Olivier a long time ago, and since then they have supported and put up with me, in all ways possible.

Translator's Acknowledgements

D AVID HOMEL WOULD like to acknowledge the assist-
ance of Alexis Leuterio.

JEAN-PAUL DUBOIS was born in 1950 in Toulouse and is a journalist and author. He won the Prix Femina for his novel *Une Vie Française*, and *Not Everybody Lives the Same Way* was awarded the Prix Goncourt in 2019. He is the author of many critically acclaimed novels and travel pieces, but he has stated that he reserves all his writing for the month of March only.

DAVID HOMEL is an author, filmmaker, journalist and literary translator from French. His translations have won numerous prizes, including the Governor General's Award for Literature, Canada's highest literary honour. He is the author of five novels, including the award-winning *The Speaking Cure*.